# THE
# ALARMING
# CAREER
## OF SIR RICHARD
# BLACKSTONE

# THE
# ALARMING
# CAREER
## OF SIR RICHARD
# BLACKSTONE

## Lisa Doan

**Sky Pony Press**
New York

Sky Pony Press books may be purchased in bulk at special discounts for sales promotion, corporate gifts, fund-raising, or educational purposes. Special editions can also be created to specifications. For details, contact the Special Sales Department, Sky Pony Press, 307 West 36th Street, 11th Floor, New York, NY 10018 or info@skyhorsepublishing.com.

Sky Pony® is a registered trademark of Skyhorse Publishing, Inc.®, a Delaware corporation.

Visit our website at www.skyponypress.com.

10 9 8 7 6 5 4 3 2 1

Library of Congress Cataloging-in-Publication Data is available on file.

Cover illustration by Chris Piascik
Cover design by Georgia Morrissey

Print ISBN: 978-1-5107-1122-8
Ebook ISBN: 978-1-5107-1123-5

Printed in the United States of America

Interior design by Joshua L. Barnaby

# THE
# ALARMING
# CAREER
# OF SIR RICHARD
# BLACKSTONE

# CHAPTER ONE

Henry slid across the slimy cobblestones of Fleet Street and cut around St. Bride's Church. It had rained the night before, and the brown sludge of filth that had been pitched out of every window coated the streets and pooled in the cracks between stones.

Henry's mother lagged behind him. She was a portly woman, as short in body as she was short in temper. Henry's father, on the other hand, was a tall and lanky man. A faster man. A man who gained upon Henry with every step.

Henry weaved in and out of the hawkers crowding the street. He dodged a boy waving copies of *The Tattletale* and shouting the headline of the day—Her Majesty's health was much improved. He zigzagged around makeshift tables piled high with oysters, men pushing barrows of kidney pie, and girls carrying baskets of eels and oranges.

Henry had been living on the streets for months, desperately searching for a way out of London. Every day of those months, his parents had dogged him throughout the

1

city. They had nearly caught him a week ago when he let down his guard while strolling along the Thames watching a ship hoist its mighty sails. Now, just when the baker had told him of a promising advertisement for work in the Hampshire countryside, his parents had spotted him again. The chase was on, and if he couldn't lose them quickly, he would miss his chance at the position.

He couldn't afford to miss it. The advertisement offered a job with pay, and that meant it wasn't an apprenticeship. He would not be bound to anybody, and those sorts of opportunities did not come along every day.

Henry's father was closing in, the soles of his leather boots slapping on the cobblestones behind him.

His father yelled, "Thief!"

Henry pumped his legs ever faster and braced himself to be tackled to the ground by citizens answering the call of thief. If they got hold of him, it would be a miracle if he ever stood again. That's what happened to thieving boys. A constable would be brought, but by the time he arrived he would find his work had been made easy. The thief would be no more. Only, his father knew that Henry wasn't a thieving boy.

Henry ducked outstretched arms. He plunged down narrow alleys and flew around twists and turns, dodging behind dilapidated buildings and jumping over wooden fences. A boy who shifted for himself on the streets knew every cranny and hidey-hole. He ran toward Ludgate Hill. If he could lose his pursuers, he might be able to apply for that job yet.

Henry glanced over his shoulder before he swung around a corner. He had lost the crowd. The address he looked for, 55 Ludgate, was straight ahead. Henry bounded up the stairs, threw the door open, and collided with a gentleman who was on his way out.

The man, sandy-haired and in his early thirties, lay sprawled on the top step. He was richly dressed in a dark green coat with large brass buttons, breeches, and polished black boots. Struggling into a sitting position, the man peered at the overturned boxes splayed across the stone stairs. A look of horror spread over his features. "He's escaped," the man cried. "The Phyllobates terribilis. He's out!"

Henry looked around him. A small yellow toad with round black eyes sat placidly on the pavement.

Henry scrambled to his feet. "Sorry to knock you over like that, sir. I'll catch your toad and you'll be good as new."

Henry stepped down to get a better look at the interesting creature. He had seen a picture of a brown toad in a book once, but never anything like this brilliant yellow. Of course, the only creatures a person was likely to see in the city were horses, rats, and stray dogs. Jimmy Jenkins—a boy who had actually lived in the country—had told him the country teemed with fox and rabbit and hedgehogs. Henry supposed that such a wondrous thing as this yellow toad might exist there too, even if Jimmy Jenkins had forgotten to tell him about it. He slowly reached out his hand.

"Don't touch it!" the man said. "It's a frog, not a toad. A poisonous dart frog from South America."

Henry yanked his hand back. "Did you say poisonous, sir?"

The gentleman dusted himself off. "I did say poisonous. He's lovely, isn't he? But on no account spook him. As a general rule, Phyllobates terribilis aren't prone to being spooked. However, this particular Phyllobates terribilis finds himself in a foreign city, and one cannot guess what he thinks of it. If I were to lose him on the streets of London and he went about poisoning people, the queen would have me hanged. She's highly suspicious of foreigners—frogs included—and would look severely upon such a creature's owner."

The frog was poisonous *and* the man was swell enough to know the queen?

"That benign-looking creature," the man said, "has got enough poison on its skin to kill twenty men."

This was getting more complicated by the minute. It was dangerous to be standing on the street while his parents were looking for him and not far off. Maybe he should just run. He could bolt to Whitechapel and lose himself in its dangerous warren of narrow streets and dark alleys.

But then he had an idea.

Henry fished his tin cup from his coat pocket and

ripped the top off one of the man's paper boxes. He crept slowly toward the frog. It stared at him with big curious eyes. Henry wondered if the creature knew that it could kill him, and then another nineteen people.

Henry gently closed the cup over top of the frog, then slid the paper underneath. He eased the cup upside down. The frog plopped onto the bottom. "Here we go, sir. We'll just put him back in his rightful box and it will all be as if it never happened."

The gentleman looked over his pile of boxes. "Ah, here it is," he said, picking up a rectangular wooden box with holes punched in the top. "I see what's happened. The latch came loose when I stumbled."

Henry flinched. The man hadn't stumbled; he had been bowled over by a street boy. Henry never could understand why kindness stung him with sadness. It had always been so with the baker; each time Mr. Clemens slipped him a penny loaf, Henry's eyes watered.

The gentleman held the box open while Henry gently slid the frog inside. The man snapped the lid shut and closed the latch. "Well now, no harm done," he said. "You're a clever chap, thinking up a solution in the heat of the moment. I imagine you're a great help to your mother and father."

At the mention of his parents, Henry felt that familiar urge to run. Run far and run fast.

"What is the matter, boy?"

"Um," Henry said, glancing behind him to be certain the recently mentioned mother and father weren't barreling down the road. "Sadly, sir, I'm an orphan."

Henry had told this lie often enough. He wished it were true. Henry's parents were cold and ruthless people. He suspected they had never wanted a child to begin with. Now, they were determined to sell him off as a chimney sweep. Henry was equally determined to escape such a fate. He had found he was not alone in that wish. There was no end of children hiding out to avoid being indentured. Some had even been bound in a contract and then escaped their masters. The boys told stories of working twelve-hour days in dark and dusty chimneys, the soot finding its way into every pore and settling into their lungs. The girls told stories from the dreaded match factory of dipping stick after stick into phosphorus until their hair began to fall out. So far Henry had eluded those horrors, but it was getting harder. His parents seemed to be getting more acquainted with his strategies for surviving on the streets and had begun appearing in the neighborhoods he frequented.

"Ah," the gentleman said, "so many children left to fend for themselves in this city. It's criminal, really." The man looked thoughtful. He stared at Henry's cup. "I am afraid that is your sole possession, is it not?"

"Except for my clothes, sir."

"And now it's ruined. You won't want to drink from that again. Alkaloid batrachotoxins are not to be fooled with."

6

"Alka-what?" Henry asked.

"The poison. The poison on the frog's skin has now been transferred to the inside of your cup." The gentleman pulled a sack from one of his boxes. "One touch of it and you would find yourself paralyzed, your heart included. Once your heart stops, the game is up. Life has come to an end. Place the cup in here, and I'll dispose of it safely. I'll need to bury it somewhere."

Henry reluctantly let go of his cup. He had not thought of losing it when he decided to use it to capture the frog. Where would he get another one? The scraps of food and drops of drink he could scrounge went into that cup. It had taken him weeks of hard labor working for a fishmonger to earn the six pence to buy it from a secondhand shop.

"But I'd have to know that you didn't have any bad habits," the man said.

Henry realized the man had been talking while he agonized over his cup. "I'm sorry, what did you say, sir?"

"I said, if I try you out as my assistant, I'd have to know I wasn't bringing a hooligan into the house. Mrs. Splunket wouldn't stand for it. It's a risk, I know, taking in a street boy. But devil take it, there's not a soul in Barton Commons who will do, and just now I've interviewed one blockhead after the next. At least you seem to know your way around a frog. I asked the last boy I interviewed if he would enjoy a job that included interesting wildlife. He said, 'As long as they taste good.' You may end up murdering us in our beds, but at least you'd be clever about it."

This was the man he had been racing to see! The advertisement by a Hampshire man engaged in scientific pursuits who looked for an assistant to help him in his work. "Sir," Henry said, "I am not a hooligan. I will work morning and night. I will never even take a break to sleep! I will hardly eat. I will never need new clothes. And—"

"Hold on, boy, before you make promises you can't keep." The man eyed Henry up and down. "You certainly do need new clothes. That coat was made for someone twice your size and has more holes than wool. You *will* sleep, all creatures must. And no boy eats only a little if he can help it. Still, you seem like an earnest young chap. We'll give it a go."

The gentleman hailed a passing carriage. "I've had enough adventures on the streets of London for one day. We shall repair to The Angel and set off directly. Barton Commons is but a day's journey out of the city." After directing the driver to take them to the posthouse, he opened the door and stepped up into the carriage. Henry raced to gather the boxes and load them into the coach. He placed the box containing the Phyllobates terribilis onto the seat, careful not to jostle the creature.

The man leaned out of the coach window and pointed to a small wooden box that still remained on the top step. "Careful with that one too," he said. "That one may sit next to the Phyllobates terribilis."

Henry cautiously picked up the box. Tiny holes had been pierced through the wood on the top and he heard a soft scratching come from inside of it. Whatever it was, it was alive.

He scrambled in next to the man and gently placed the box next to the Phyllobates terribilis.

"I'm Sir Richard Blackstone, by the by," the man said, looking intently at the two boxes that sat across from him.

"Henry Hewitt, sir."

The coach started off. Henry heard a shout behind the carriage. A shout he recognized all too well. He turned to see his father jogging down the road. "Stop!" his father cried. "Stop that coach!"

Henry sank down in his seat.

"I don't know that man," Sir Richard said to the driver and waved him on. "Another lunatic carousing free in the streets, I suppose. This entire metropolis is bedlam."

By the time the coach barreled down Pentonville Road, Henry had the courage to peek out the window. His father was gone.

The courtyard of The Angel bustled with hostlers wrangling horses into harnesses and passengers fighting to get off a mail coach against a sea of passengers determined to get on. Henry followed Sir Richard through the posthouse while the arrangements were made to depart London for Hampshire. Sir Richard had directed Henry that he was to carry the two boxes, one with the Phyllobates terribilis and the other containing he knew not what. A hostler would transfer the other packages, but Henry was not to let anyone touch the two boxes. He held them away from his body in case a latch might suddenly spring open and some creature make a leap at him.

He was going to the country. The blessed country! Henry did not have any firsthand knowledge about the countryside, other than what Jimmy Jenkins had told him. When he had first met him, Jimmy had said that just as London was covered in soot, so the countryside was covered in greenery. Henry had not believed it; the whole idea had sounded fantastical. Jimmy had taken him across the city to a fancy neighborhood and introduced him to Hyde Park. There, they had run along the paths and around the trees and through acres of greenery until they were chased out by a constable. From what Henry had seen of Hyde Park, he now knew that such a landscape of green was possible; it just seemed incredible that he should be able to go live in it.

They were led to a private room and Sir Richard ordered food. Henry carefully set down the boxes on the chair next to him and dove into sausages, slurped down oysters, and took large bites of fresh-baked bread slathered in butter. Sir Richard eyed him and said, "Yes, I see what you mean. You eat like a bird."

Henry slowly laid down a forkful of sausage. He had already forgotten that he had promised not to eat very much.

Sir Richard laughed and said, "Carry on, Henry. We are not short of food at the manor—Mrs. Splunket sees to that. I expect she'll be pleased to have somebody about the place who has a real enthusiasm for it."

Henry was on his way to a manor. A manor was not just a regular house, it was practically a castle. He would work for a sir, not an everyday mister. A wonderful woman named Mrs. Splunket lived there and liked a person to be enthusiastic about food. Henry guessed that he and Mrs. Splunket would get on famously.

After Henry had demolished the rest of his sausage and ensured that the only clues that a loaf of bread had once been on the table were the tiniest of crumbs, they made their way to the courtyard.

A smart-looking chaise pulled by four matched bay horses pulled up in front of the inn.

Even though Sir Richard was a knight, Henry had not expected a private carriage. He had assumed they waited for the next mail coach. Sir Richard would be squeezed in with a crowd of other people who were able to pay for the privilege. Henry would be hanging on somewhere outside. He had heard all about it from the baker. Mr. Clemens said that riding in a mail coach didn't kill a person, it just made a person wish to be killed.

A stocky man, squeezed into green and white livery like one of the pork sausages Henry had just eaten, tipped his hat to Sir Richard. The coachman stared at Henry.

**11**

"Ah, Bertram," Sir Richard said. "This is my new assistant, Henry Hewitt."

Bertram looked down his short, pudgy nose and eyed Henry's coat full of holes and his grimy face. The coachman narrowed his eyes with suspicion.

"Get on with you," Sir Richard said to Bertram. "Yes, you highly disapprove, I can see that. Fortunately, it was never your decision."

Bertram seemed satisfied that his feelings were so well known without his having to speak them. He nodded and opened the door to the chaise.

Sir Richard climbed in. Henry attempted to go in after him, but Bertram grabbed him by the collar and said, "You ride outside."

"Don't be ridiculous, Bertram," Sir Richard called from inside the coach. "There's room for four people in here. I'd let *you* in if you weren't driving the horses."

Bertram reluctantly let Henry go and muttered, "Them is leather seats in there. Who's to be cleaning the London soot off of 'em afterwards? Only myself."

Henry climbed in and sat on the bench next to Sir Richard. He set the two boxes on the seat across from him and pushed them against the backrest. He picked up a blanket he found folded up in a corner and placed it in front of the boxes so they wouldn't tumble off if the coach hit any bumps in the road.

Sir Richard looked over Henry's handiwork and said, "I see what you've done. Clever."

The carriage made its way through the crowded London streets. However unpleasant Bertram was, he was a skilled driver. He weaved around farmers' carts, hansom cabs, and pedestrians, and shouted out insults when something or someone refused to move out of the way.

Henry leaned back, making certain that his face was away from the window. He was close to a new life, but it would be quickly undone if he were spotted by his mother or father.

They cleared the outskirts of the city. Henry did not think his parents would look for him in Hampshire. It was true that he had more than once overheard that county mentioned when they argued, but he had never heard them talk of going back to it.

Now that the danger had passed, Henry began to enjoy the scenery. He stared at the open fields. So much space to move around in! The horses trotted through a wood; tall oaks stretched their heavy branches over a narrow lane. They passed a farmer who tipped his cap to the coach, and then laughed when Henry enthusiastically waved. But what struck Henry the most was the air. It didn't smell of sulphur and smoke. It smelled clean. That was something he could not have known from his trip to Hyde Park. Until this moment, Henry had thought the air of the whole world was gray and thick; now he knew otherwise.

They stopped once to change the horses. Hostlers raced to unhitch one team and lead another into place, and the good woman who owned the inn tried her best to tempt them inside for a meal and a glass of ale. But Sir Richard would not even get out of the chaise to stretch his legs. He was engrossed in his books and occasionally muttered, "I see, of course that would be it," before scribbling furiously on a bit of parchment.

In the early evening, Sir Richard put his books away. "We're nearly there," he said as he joined Henry in watching the countryside roll by. "We are but a quarter mile from the turnoff to Barton Commons."

# CHAPTER TWO

Blackstone Manor was a towering limestone structure of two stories. A row of stately columns lined a front portico with tall mahogany doors at its center. Glazed windows taller than a man ran the length of the house. A wide cobblestone courtyard was fronted by a well-tended rose garden. Henry thought it was very like a drawing of a castle he had once seen on a playbill.

Bertram opened the coach door and once more gave Henry as dour a look as he could manage. The coachman seemed determined to express his ardent disapproval of Henry being hired as an assistant, of Henry riding inside the coach, and of Henry in general.

A wonderfully round woman with pink cheeks and bright blue eyes hurried down the steps. As Sir Richard descended, she peered over his shoulder and into the coach. "Ah, sir, you have found your boy!"

Sir Richard nodded. Bertram muttered, "Such as he is."

Mrs. Splunket turned to Bertram and said, "Mind your

business, you miserable old thing." She held a hand out to Henry and helped him out of the coach. "Don't you mind Bertram. Yes, I can see why he's cross—you are filthy and badly dressed. No worries, we shall have that fixed in under an hour. If Sir Richard says you're all right, then you are all right in my book. Some people," she said, glancing over her shoulder at Bertram, "would do well to think likewise."

"This is Henry Hewitt, Mrs. Splunket," Sir Richard said. He had carried the two boxes from the coach, one under each arm. "I'll leave the boy to your capable hands, as I have two other charges who must be cared for."

Mrs. Splunket eyed the boxes. "Do I want to ask what's inside them?" she said.

"I think not," Sir Richard said.

"Will you at least assure me that it's not more of them evil little fish that bite?" Mrs. Splunket asked.

Henry had never heard of fish that bite. If he had, he would never have ventured into the Thames to cool off or wash himself.

"You may be easy on that point, Mrs. Splunket," Sir Richard said. "It is not more piranhas."

"Thank heavens for that. I'll have the boy sorted out directly," Mrs. Splunket said.

Mrs. Splunket led Henry to the kitchen and heated water for a bath. After she filled the tub, she handed Henry strong soap and ordered him to scrub the soot of London off his person. When he was certain he was clean, he was to scrub again.

"You'll find new clothes right there, dear," Mrs. Splunket said. A pile of clothing was folded neatly on the table.

"I would attempt to wash what you're wearing," Mrs. Splunket said, looking at his clothes, "but I think they'd be better off burned. We don't need fleas in the house."

"But not my shoes," Henry said with alarm. He had to always wear his shoes.

"If you're set on keeping them, I don't see why not. Though you'll find shoes and stockings ready for you with the rest of it."

Henry was relieved. He could not let anyone, ever, see his feet. They were his secret and that was the way it must stay.

"I'll just leave you now," Mrs. Splunket said. "Find me in my little nook around the corner when you're done."

Henry waited until Mrs. Splunket had left before removing his shoes. He lowered himself into the warm water and scrubbed, and then scrubbed again. It seemed as if years of dirt came off his person and the water turned a murky gray. The last time he'd had a bath was weeks ago when he had dared walk into the Thames wearing his clothes in an attempt to clean himself. As a person never knew what might float by on the Thames, including unfortunate individuals who had ended up in it, he had not stayed long. He supposed he could only be grateful that he had not known of piranhas, as that would have added an extra fright to the experience.

After the bath, Henry put on his new clothes. They were of fine material and included trousers, a cambric shirt, a waistcoat, and a jacket to go over it all. He hurriedly pulled on his socks and boots and felt more relaxed when his feet were covered.

Henry found Mrs. Splunket in her housekeeper's nook. It was a small closet fitted out with a desk and chair and she showed him how she filed her recipes and made her lists for shopping and did her inventory of the cupboards. There was more to housekeeping, she said, than most people understood.

After tea and buttered toast, Mrs. Splunket told him that while he was in the bath, she'd had a conference with Sir Richard on the nature of Henry's employment. Sir Richard had wondered where Henry should sleep. Mrs. Splunket informed him that bedchambers were the usual place. Sir Richard had wondered where Henry should eat. Mrs. Splunket pointed out that they had a dining room for that very activity. Sir Richard had wondered what he should have Henry do first. Mrs. Splunket delivered her firm opinion that what Henry should do first was sleep. Sir Richard had finally stopped wondering about everything and left it up to Mrs. Splunket to make the arrangements. As far as Henry could tell, he was to live inside the manor almost like he was a gentleman himself, and he was not to do any work until the morrow. And it was all thanks to Mrs. Splunket.

Before she led him upstairs, Mrs. Splunket showed Henry the first floor. The dining room where he would take his meals was astounding to Henry's eyes. A long, polished wood table ran the center of it, flanked at each end by a marble fireplace. Even though nobody was in the room, crystal chandeliers winked with dozens of wax candles. Silk wall hangings depicting hunting scenes covered the cold, rough-hewn stone of the manor walls. Henry had never imagined that he would be allowed to enter such a place, much less sit down and eat in it.

Just at the bottom of the staircase, they passed a mysterious room. Henry supposed it had once been a drawing room, though now it was filled with all manner of scientific equipment and a strange fog hung in the air. Henry could barely see Sir Richard's tall silhouette pacing through the mist.

Henry was installed in a large bedchamber on the second floor. Until Mrs. Splunket had taken charge of the arrangements, he had assumed he would sleep under a table in the kitchen, or on a bale of hay in the stables. Now he found that he had an entire room of his own. Everything about it was big. The windows soared toward the ceiling and the sills wide enough to sit upon. The bed might comfortably hold five people, and the mantle over the fireplace was so high he would have to stand on his toes to reach it. It had been his dearest wish to find some small place to sleep indoors, and now he was in a room that a duke wouldn't turn his nose up at.

Mrs. Splunket lit the fire while Henry hurriedly climbed in bed. He slid his boots off out of her view and kept his stockings on.

Mrs. Splunket pulled the coverlet up under his chin and said, "Come to the kitchen in the morning and I'll cook you a good old English fry-up." She blew out the candle and shut the door.

Henry stayed up for hours, afraid if he closed his eyes he would wake up in a back alley of London. It seemed almost too good to be true. He had done it! He had escaped the city and his grasping parents and a life of misery as a chimney sweep. Sir Richard seemed to be a kind employer and Mrs. Splunket was already one of his favorite people. Bertram didn't like him, he knew that, but he thought he might win the man over with time. He drifted off wondering what a good old English fry-up might be.

Henry woke with the sun as it shone through the tall windows that lined the room. He was still here. It had not been a dream. He jumped down from the bed onto the thick Persian rug and glanced at his still-stockinged feet. He would have to make sure nobody saw his toes. They could ruin everything.

He struggled into his new clothes and ran down to the

kitchen. As he ate his way through a rasher of bacon, five sausages, two fried eggs, and three fried kidneys, Mrs. Splunket said, "It's about time there was somebody 'round here that appreciates a good fry-up. Now let's see what you can do to a stack of fried bread and a pot of strong tea."

Once Mrs. Splunket was thoroughly convinced that Henry could not swallow another fried crumb, she sent him to Sir Richard.

The door to the mysterious room he had passed the night before was closed. Henry tapped on it.

"Enter," Sir Richard called out.

Henry pushed open the door. Tables were lined against the walls and stacked with beakers, burners, and haphazardly piled parchments. Glass aquariums sat in a line, most of them empty. Henry spotted the Phyllobates terribilis sitting placidly in the corner aquarium and an enormous, hairy spider attempting to climb the walls of another. He supposed the spider was what occupied the other box he had carried the day before. Between them, a burner heating a pot of water sent steam into the air, creating a fog and giving the air a humid feel. The inner wall of the room was lined with floor-to-ceiling bookshelves, filled to overflowing with leather-bound books. Pots filled with unusual-looking plants sat near the window.

"My laboratory," Sir Richard said. "I'm a man of science and quite determined to make discoveries. That is the only way humankind can progress and prosper."

"Yes, sir," Henry said, glancing at the pot of boiling water. "Shall I take that off the flame, sir? Is it for tea?"

Sir Richard laughed. "That is certainly not for tea. By boiling the water I attempt to replicate the humidity that would be found in the Amazon jungle. I like my creatures to feel at home."

"Yes, sir," Henry said, casting about for something to do. "Would you like me to straighten up the place for you?"

"Good grief, don't move anything or I'll never find it again. No, in order for you to assist me with my research, you'll have to learn to read. I'll advertise for a tutor. In the meantime, you can use my books to look at the pictures. One can often learn quite a bit from drawings."

"I can read, sir."

"Can you?" Sir Richard said, with a note of surprise. "How comes an orphan to reading?"

Henry wasn't sure how he had come to reading. His parents had sent him to school for two years. He had done very well, but then they had suddenly announced they would send him out to work instead. That was when he had run. He knew what happened to children who were sent out to work. The young girl in the apartment above him had phossy jaw from working in a match factory. Henry had often heard her moan through the night and the exposed bone on her face was hard not to stare at. He did not understand why his parents had bothered sending him to school in the first place if they had intended all along to send him out to work.

"My mother and father sent me to school, sir."

"Ah," Sir Richard said, nodding, "they must have had big plans for you before they were carried off. A pity, but that does make things simpler. See that book lying on the table? It's about the creatures of the Amazon. Educate yourself, and then you may begin assisting me with my experiments."

Though Henry had been taught to read, it had been some time since he had done so. Slowly, he sounded out the words. *Megasoma elephas* was also called the rhino beetle. The males used their long horns for fighting. Despite their small size, they were able to lift up to eight hundred and fifty times their own weight.

The *Hydrochoerus hydrochaeris*, or capybara, was the largest rodent in the world and could weigh as much as a man. It was known to be a good swimmer and used the water to escape predators, like the jaguar.

The *Eunectes murinus*, the green anaconda, had a body as wide in diameter as a stovepipe. They were not poisonous, but Henry didn't think that made things any better, since the snake liked to constrict and drown its prey, which could be as big as a deer.

Piranhas, or *Pygocentrus nattereri*, had teeth that looked as if they had been filed to sharp points. They would devour anything that fell into the water and could get so enthusiastic that they ended up accidentally devouring each other. Henry discovered that the Thames was not a natural habitat for these small fish that bite. Sir Richard noticed him looking at the picture of the fish and told him he had a marvelous collection of them in the fountain at the back of the house. "Just don't wave any of your fingers near the water," Sir Richard said. "They are perfectly capable of leaping up and relieving you of them."

Henry began to get the idea that if one were to be wandering around the Amazon jungle, one had better watch where they stepped and stay out of the water.

"A hybrid!" Sir Richard cried. "Of course, why didn't I see it before?"

Henry dropped his book and ran to Sir Richard. Sir Richard circled a small pot holding a plant growing low to the ground with teardrop-shaped leaves. The leaves appeared to be dotted with dew.

"What is it, sir?" Henry asked.

"That is a sundew. Very interesting plant. You see those little drops? An insect will be attracted to them, then the insect will become caught, as it's sticky. Then what do you suppose the sundew does?"

"I don't know, sir," Henry said. It had never occurred to him that a plant did anything about anything.

"The leaf that holds the trapped insect will fold in on itself and release digestive enzymes to devour the insect."

"The plant eats bugs?" Henry asked.

"Indeed," Sir Richard answered.

Henry thought that was a fairly horrifying idea. If the plant could decide to eat something, then the plant must be thinking. He wondered if trees could think.

"Fascinating as the sundew's methods are," Sir Richard said, "that is not what has captured my imagination just now. Remember, Henry, the goal we're after is to improve the lives of our fellow man. What bothers people in the summer? Flies. What does every English garden grow? Roses. You see? I shall simply cross the sundew with a rose bush and create a hybrid rose that eats flies. Great heavens, amateur botanists are always creating hybrid roses and naming them after themselves, but what do those hybrids actually do?"

"Probably just look nice, sir?" Henry said.

"Precisely," Sir Richard said. "They just sit there looking nice. While our rose, the Blackstone Fly Eliminator, will rid every English garden of annoying pests. I'll just get a shovel, dig up one of the rose bushes from the front garden, and we will be on our way to making history."

Sir Richard spent weeks trying to create the Blackstone Fly Eliminator with no success. He carefully pollinated the rose bush, then when that didn't work he blamed it on that particular rose bush and dug up another. At the end of it, the front garden had been transformed into a series of holes. He finally concluded that English roses were stubborn and unwillingly to learn a new way of doing things.

Sir Richard's mind was distracted from the stubborn roses when a pony arrived for Henry. Sir Richard had written to a friend who bred horses and the gentleman had sent along a gray-colored Welsh pony with a note that said, *Don't be put off by the name (Cantankerous). He is a sturdy little beast and will get you wherever you're going.*

Bertram had been assigned to give Henry riding lessons. This seemed doubly a challenge, as Henry was already frightened of Cantankerous, who had bitten him on arrival, and was leery of Bertram, who seemed always on the verge of biting him.

Bertram had saddled up the pony and helped Henry mount, all the while muttering, "I'm a coachman. Does this look like a carriage? No, it don't."

Henry gripped the reins tight.

"Don't pull on him, now," Bertram scolded. "He'll fight against it."

Henry loosened the reins, though it seemed like a bad idea. He didn't have anything else to hold on to.

"I suppose I better teach you right," Bertram said, "else I'll get blamed."

Henry figured that was as good a reason as any.

"You'll want to control the horse with your legs. That's how you'll tell it where you want to go. It ain't like driving a carriage, mind, as *that* takes real skill and experience."

"All right," Henry said, "so if I want to go right, I press my right leg?"

"I don't know!" Bertram shouted. "It depends on how the horse was schooled. Who rode him before? How did they teach him?"

Cantankerous began to rear his head at all the shouting. He backed up, as if to get away from Bertram. Henry tightened the reins.

Cantankerous bucked and Henry found himself lying on the ground.

Bertram looked down at him and said, "That looks less like ridin' and more like falling off. You're gonna have to get right back on him or he won't never let you ride him again."

Henry climbed back on Cantankerous, though his every instinct told him not to. His instincts had been correct, as he was thrown off three more times. As much as Bertram tried to maintain his gruff exterior, he became more amused each time Henry hit the ground. He even began to warm a little as Henry asked him questions about horses.

Bertram said nobody knew the species better than he did. He had an uncanny knack with animals in general and when an animal saw Bertram, it thought, *Now here's a man I can't fool with.*

After the third fall, Bertram explained to Henry that he was locked in a battle of wills with the pony and whoever gave up first would be the loser forevermore. Henry climbed back on, and Cantankerous finally allowed himself to be ridden around the paddock. Despite the win, Bertram could give no guarantee about what Cantankerous might do tomorrow, as he said there was never a stubborner creature than a bad-tempered pony.

As the weeks passed by, Henry quickly adjusted to being Sir Richard's assistant. One of his jobs was to feed the frog and the tarantula each day. He had named the frog Mr. Terrible, for Terribilis and for the fact that it could accidentally kill twenty men. The tarantula's genus was Theraphosa, but Sir Richard could find no evidence that this particular species had been previously discovered. He named the spider Theraphosa nigrum lapis, using the Latin words for black and stone. He had written to the Norwich Natural History Society to apprise them of that fact, in case any of the members were to lay their hands on a similar tarantula and attempt to name it after themselves. Henry did not think Theraphosa nigrum lapis really described the spider's personality and decided to call her Mary, Queen of Scots, for her impetuous nature. She was forever boldly attempting to climb the aquarium glass, though if she got out no good could come of it. Sir Richard had said there were people like that—never satisfied with where they were and always certain the grass was greener somewhere else.

Henry also fed the piranhas every day and, once he

became used to them, found he enjoyed throwing a hunk of meat into the pond and watching the water roil as the beasts devoured it.

Henry's biggest job, though, was cheering up Sir Richard when an experiment failed. Sir Richard had never said that was part of Henry's job, but Henry began to think it was needed and talked it over with Mrs. Splunket. They both agreed that Sir Richard took his failures too much to heart and needed to be distracted when things went wrong, which was always. Mrs. Splunket said that if Sir Richard were to line up all his failures in a row and have a long and hard look at them, he'd give up experiments altogether.

After the sundew-roses hybrid came to nothing, the knight had moved on. He built himself a pair of wings from wood and parchment and jumped off a fence post. But instead of gliding across the field as he had envisioned, he now walked with a limp. He had spent days tinkering with how to invent a smokeless fireplace, until their clothes were permeated with the smell of burned wood. He had even been so bold as to attempt to train deer to carry letters and messages, the theory being they could take shortcuts through the woods instead of always having to go along roads. Their very efficiency could put the postal service out of business. Sir Richard had only managed to catch one deer and whatever letters he had packed in a small satchel around the animal's neck were deep in the forest by now. Sir Richard remained convinced that particular experiment could be made to work if confined to only two points of geography with food for the animal at either end. Unfortunately, they had failed to set up a second point for the deer to aim for.

Sir Richard often sent Henry off on errands to deliver a message or pick up something for Mrs. Splunket. Henry got to know the neighborhood, which he thought was very elegant. A duchess, cousin to the queen herself, lived right next door. The village of Barton Commons was just down the road. He met the local shopkeeper, the barman at the tavern, the blacksmith, and plenty of local farmers. More than once he was told that he didn't seem the rough urchin they had heard about. Henry assumed he could thank Bertram for that.

Henry continued his lessons on Cantankerous and managed to take him across a few fields, but the pony was diabolical. Cantankerous specialized in the unpredictable and seemed to know exactly the moment when Henry had let down his guard. He might rear up, he might sidestep, he might go backwards, he might come to a sudden stop, or his teeth might lunge at Henry's leg. Henry supposed he had not even seen all of the pony's tricks and was generally relieved to put the horse in his stall and return to the manor. His first stop after riding was usually the kitchen, as there was always something cooking that would cheer him up after his battle with Cantankerous.

Weeks passed and Henry and Mrs. Splunket grew very comfortable together. When he wasn't doing something for Sir Richard, Henry lounged in the kitchen and ate cakes and thick strips of fried bacon. He got used to not feeling hungry all the time, and he gained weight and grew stronger by the day.

Mrs. Splunket was a widow and told Henry that her late husband, Mr. Camus Splunket, had met with an untimely end while pole vaulting over a barn on a wager. She said Mr. Splunket had not been overrun with brains, and what little brains he'd had were left scattered on the ground. When Henry appeared grieved by this sad tale, she said, "Never mind, dearie, he's pole vaulting over clouds now."

At night, Henry lit a candle on his bedside table and snuggled into his bed with a book he had borrowed from Sir Richard's library. There was a particular collection of stories he liked, filled with dragons and princesses and knights. The dragons were fearsome, but the knights were honorable and brave and the princesses were always kind. The people in the book were so different from the people he had encountered on the streets of London. Londoners might rob a person while they weren't looking or even murder a person in their sleep. Maybe they would get caught, maybe they wouldn't. In the book, evildoers always got caught and the knights always won. He usually drifted off with the book on his chest.

In the mornings, when Henry opened his eyes and looked around his room—with its cozy carpets and a cheerful fire burning in the grate—he gave thanks that providence had sent Sir Richard his way. The gentleman was odd, conducting strange experiments that never resulted in anything, but he was kind. Very kind.

One late afternoon, Henry crouched in a corner of Sir Richard's laboratory, arranging scientific journals by date. Sir Richard was particularly interested in the handwritten journals of his friend, John Fitzwilliam, detailing a year spent exploring the Amazon jungle. Fitzwilliam had brought back some live—and some dead—species he had encountered and had given Sir Richard Mr. Terrible, Mary, Queen of Scots, the piranhas, and the creepy sundew plant.

The aquariums lining the wall reflected the light of the setting sun; Henry could just make out Mr. Terrible perched on a rock in his corner. The hiss of steam from the boiling kettle permeated the room.

Sir Richard stood at a table working on some new experiment. Henry heard him swear. The door slammed and the room grew quiet. Then the front door slammed. Henry smiled. Another one of his master's experiments had ended with a walk in the front garden (now reduced to holes) to clear his thoughts and calm his temper. Henry would have to do his very best to cheer up Sir Richard over dinner.

Henry heard the front door open again. He wondered at it, as Sir Richard's walks after a failure usually lasted at least an hour.

Sir Richard burst back into the laboratory and said, "I've had experiments go wrong before, but this is a real corker."

Henry stood up. "What's happened, sir?"

"What's happened?" Sir Richard asked. "Look out the window."

Henry peered past the table overflowing with books and beakers toward the leaded glass bay windows. A spiky black tree had sprouted up in front of the middle glass. "Ah," Henry said, nodding, "you've been experimenting with horticulture again. Another hybrid. Is it not exactly what you wanted, sir? Shall I chop it down directly?"

"Chop it down directly? It could chop you down directly!"

Henry glanced back at the window. The spiky black tree had moved. "Sir," Henry said, "what is that exactly? You haven't invented a tree that can walk, have you?"

"That's no tree, Henry. That's the Theraphosa nigrum lapis. The more pressing question is, where is she going? If she heads toward the duchess's annual dusk-to-dawn croquet party, I shall never hear the end of it."

Henry spun around to the table behind him. The aquarium that had recently held Mary, Queen of Scots, was empty. "Sir, was that Mr. Fitzwilliam's tarantula? *That* Theraphosa nigrum lapis? But how could she get so big?"

"How should I know?" Sir Richard said, in a voice that sounded an octave higher than usual. "I used a little of this and a little of that and added something else, then I noticed that instead of her turning yellow as I had planned—because yellow is the queen's favorite color and her birthday is coming up—she was getting bigger and I thought, *now that's unexpected*, then she got alarmingly big, so I threw her outside, and she just kept growing." Sir Richard stared down at the table filled with pots and beakers of ingredients. "Don't move anything—something here has caused this catastrophe."

Henry stared at Sir Richard. "Wait, you thought the queen would like a yellow tarantula for her birthday?" Henry asked.

"I can't say whether she'd like it, I just know she hasn't got one already. Blast it, where has that spider gone?"

Henry looked. Where *had* she gone?

# CHAPTER THREE

"**S**words and horses," Sir Richard said.

"What?"

"Swords and horses! Run to the stable and direct Bertram to saddle up Real Beauty and Cantankerous. I'll get the swords. The duchess's dusk-to-dawn croquet party is set to begin at any moment. We've got to waylay that spider before she devours a debutante, mallet and all."

Henry didn't know how he would manage a sword on horseback. He had never used a sword in his life and was only just beginning to be able to stay on Cantankerous with two hands on the reins.

Henry raced out the kitchen door, looking in both directions to make sure the tarantula was not hovering nearby. He spotted Mary swaying and wobbling near the front of the manor. Henry supposed she was trying to get used to her bigger legs. Considering there were eight, he hoped it would take awhile.

He dashed across the yard to the stable. "Bertram," he

called, "saddle up Real Beauty and Cantankerous. Sir Richard wants to . . . go for a ride."

Bertram lay on a bale of hay chewing on a stalk and staring at the rafters. He hauled himself up and strode away mumbling, "No regular schedule with this one. Most decent folk don't go willy-nilly wanting to ride and then not wanting to ride. A fellow can hardly relax when he don't know what's coming next."

Henry peeked out the stable door. Two of the tarantula's eight legs were visible from around the corner of the manor. Hopefully, Bertram wouldn't notice. He still complained about how he had nearly lost a finger while sitting next to the fountain stocked with Fitzwilliam's piranhas.

Sir Richard burst out of the kitchen garden gate as Bertram led out the horses. He threw a sword to Henry and grabbed Real Beauty's reins. "Bertram, should you happen to see a largish spider, my advice is *run*."

Bertram turned on his heel, muttering, "As if a grown man is afeared of spiders!"

Sir Richard mounted his chestnut horse and said, "We don't have much time. Once that creature smells the duchess's cucumber sandwiches, she will head right for them."

Henry struggled onto Cantankerous. The metal sword was heavy in his right hand and he had his doubts about being able to control the pony with only one hand on the reins. Cantankerous seemed to have doubts of his own and tried to bite Henry's leg by way of comment. The pony missed

Henry's calf but snorted, as if to say, "Don't relax, I'll try that again."

Henry settled himself into the saddle and balanced his sword across his lap. "What's the plan, sir?" he asked Sir Richard.

"If we can get ahead of her, we may be able to back her into the forest, but we must be careful. Those hairs on her abdomen are urticating bristles—consider them barbed arrows. Should you see her kick out with her back legs, duck. Then, there are the chelicerae to watch out for; the venom in the fangs of a spider of that size would be lethal. The claws would not normally cause concern, but in their current state they could rip a person's head off."

Henry was just going to figure that the entire tarantula was dangerous.

"Don't be put off by all those eyes, Henry. Yes, eight is more eyes than we are accustomed to, but her vision is not sharp. Movement and vibration are what the creature will rely on."

"It'll be full dark soon, sir."

The sun had already sunk below the oaks of the Queen's Forest. Points of light sprung up across the duchess's lawn. The lady's footmen scurried back and forth, lighting torches for night-time croquet.

"Quickly, Henry, she's on the move!"

Mary, Queen of Scots, lumbered down the slope toward the lights, as if she were on the guest list for the duchess's annual dusk-to-dawn croquet party. Getting used to her bigger legs hadn't taken as long as Henry had hoped.

Sir Richard spurred Real Beauty into a gallop. Henry spurred Cantankerous, cursed him, pleaded with him, wrestled his pant leg out of the pony's mouth, and eventually galloped behind Sir Richard.

The tarantula was halfway down the hill already and gravity gave her momentum. As they approached her, Henry got a closer look.

Her body had grown to the size of a mail coach, comprised of two round parts connected in the middle. Her legs were the height of a tall man. Her claws looked like curved black daggers attached to hairy handles.

The tarantula hovered in the shadows, her massive outline showed against the torch flames. She paused, as if trying to understand what she saw through her eight bleary eyes.

Ladies in pastel ball gowns swung mallets at wooden croquet balls. Gentlemen in tailcoats cheered them on. The duchess's staff, dressed in starched blue and white livery, wound around the players and passed glasses of champagne from silver trays to outstretched hands. A long table covered in white linen was piled high with the duchess's renowned cucumber sandwiches.

Mary reached out with one of her forelegs and swept a tray of sandwiches to the ground. The table swayed and tumbled over.

The crash rang through the night. The croquet game halted and a footman ran toward the sound.

Mary, Queen of Scots, raised herself up.

The footman staggered back. "What is that?" he cried.

"The torches, sir," Henry called. He threw down his sword and wheeled Cantankerous toward the nearest torch, pulling the post from the ground. It was heavy and awkward.

"Good thinking," Sir Richard yelled. "We shall fire-joust her into the forest!"

Sir Richard grabbed the torch on the far side of the over-turned table. The tarantula backed farther into the night. The reflection of the flames danced in her glassy eyes. Henry held the torch like a javelin and charged forward.

"That's it, Henry, fear nothing," Sir Richard called, wheeling around to the other side. "Simply watch for the chelicerae, the claws, and the urticating hairs. Otherwise, she can't do a thing to you!"

Henry jabbed his torch at the tarantula, hoping to scare her into a retreat. Mary spun around and lifted her back legs. He ducked as a slew of black arrows flew over his head.

The tarantula lumbered away and Henry drove Cantankerous after it. The pony decided it wished to go in any direction except the spider's, and Henry found himself zigzagging across the lawn as he desperately pulled on the reins.

Behind him, he heard the duchess's commanding voice call out, "Richard Blackstone!"

Henry neared the tarantula and waved his torch at the creature's back legs. He sensed that she didn't like the light or the heat.

The Theraphosa nigrum lapis stumbled toward the forest. Sir Richard and Henry chased it from behind, waving the torches at its legs until Mary disappeared into the woods.

Henry and Sir Richard reined in their mounts as they neared the old oaks that marked the edge of the Queen's Forest. "Go no farther, Henry," Sir Richard called.

Henry was relieved. In the daylight, the Queen's Forest was a cheerful kind of place full of deer, rabbits, birdsong, and babbling brooks. At night though, the forest took on an ominous look, dark and brooding as if it could swallow a person up. He would not dare go in, even if there weren't a giant tarantula stumbling around. He had not grown so used to country life as that.

Sir Richard clapped him on the back. "Good work. I daresay the duchess's guests did not notice too terribly much."

Henry looked back to the croquet lawn. The guests had deserted. Footmen scrambled to douse torches and haul the tables inside.

Sir Richard surveyed the scene. "Well. That's unfortunate."

"Sir," Henry said, "we should probably go back and get my sword and the barbs Mary shot at me."

"The urticating bristles! Good thinking, Henry. It would not do to have those found in the morning."

They turned their horses and made their way back to the lawn. Henry watched the last of the footmen scramble into the house. He heard the distant sounds of carriages being called for and guessed that the duchess's guests were not wasting a moment before being on their way home. Mary had completely wrecked the lady's party and he was sure Sir Richard would hear of it. Just as well that his master would not find himself explaining where the urticating bristles came from.

It did not take long to locate the barbs—they had landed in the soft earth like javelins. Henry collected his sword while Sir Richard pulled the barbs from the ground.

As they rode back toward the house, Sir Richard said, "I'll pitch them in the piranha pond. Nobody will stick their hand in there to find out what's in it."

After Henry had washed the sweat and dirt from his face, he went down to the dining room. Mrs. Splunket lumbered in, pushing a rolling cart piled high with food. She set grilled fish, fried oysters, a roast pheasant, a sliced onion, baked apples, a hearty loaf of wheat bread, and a pitcher of ale onto the table. From her manner, it was clear she did not know that he and Sir Richard had been out of the house or that anything had gone amiss at the duchess's party. Weeks ago, she had told Henry she was disappointed that Sir Richard chose not to attend the duchess's dusk-to-dawn croquet party. She had said, "Them two go together like a fork and a spoon. If he would only see it." Now she laid the table while softly talking to herself. "It's just a shame, is what it is. A fine lady hosts a fancy party and a knight who lives right next door don't go."

Henry thought she seemed as disappointed as ever that Sir Richard didn't see that he and the duchess went together like silverware.

"One can't help feelin' sorry over it," she said.

Sir Richard pretended he didn't hear her.

After she retired, Henry leaned over and said in a low voice, "Do you think Mary will stay in the forest?"

Sir Richard waved a fried oyster on his fork. "No doubt, my boy. If you were a Theraphosa nigrum lapis creeping around the Amazon jungle and been suddenly swept up, put on a boat to England, dropped off at a manor house, called Mary, Queen of Scots, and expected to turn yellow, only to find that you were now hundreds of times bigger, then made an unsuccessful run at some cucumber sandwiches and been driven off by torches, wouldn't *you* stay in the forest? The more pertinent question is what the duchess will say, and that will depend a great deal on what she actually saw. Thank heaven that awful Snidefellow wasn't about. There's nothing that man likes more than stirring up trouble."

Henry had only seen Mr. Snidefellow once, when he and Sir Richard had gone to the village to pick up supplies for Mrs. Splunket. Sir Richard had met Snidefellow on the road and had later told Henry that Snidefellow was a councilman. Fifty years before, tenant farmers across England had united, surrounding their landowners' estates, waving pitchforks and demanding better terms. The nobility had been terrified and the crown had speedily created the role of councilmen—men appointed by local nobles—to see that there was no repetition of what was later called The Great Pitchfork Rebellion. Since that time, the councilmen had expanded their role and now monitored both secular and religious activities and had broad power to arrest and prosecute as they saw fit. London had been full of them and Henry had been careful to stay out of their way. He had heard that the men had quotas of people to be delivered to the workhouse, as it was their responsibility to keep beggars off the streets. They preferred children because children were easier to subdue.

That day they had come upon the councilman on the road, he had bowed stiffly and said, "Sir Richard, shall we ever have the pleasure of seeing you at a church service one of these fine mornings?"

Sir Richard had been distracted and said, "No, my good fellow, not today, I'm in a bit of a hurry."

Mr. Snidefellow had raised a thin and scraggly brow and said, "Today is Tuesday. Church services occur on Sunday. Every Sunday. It's somewhat of a tradition."

Now, Henry said, "Yes, sir, Mr. Snidefellow doesn't seem like the sort of person who would approve of a giant tarantula."

Sir Richard nodded and raised his glass. "Here's to clever companions who grab torches in the nick of time. The boy saves the night and knight. Get it? Save the night, meaning this evening, and save the knight, meaning me?"

Henry flushed and clinked glasses with Sir Richard. He had always promised himself that if he could get any real work, he would do it better than anybody would expect. So far, he had mainly spent his time cheering up his employer. Now, he felt like he had really done something to help Sir Richard.

"Sir," Henry said, thinking this might be a good time to ask something he had wondered about since he had arrived at the manor, "how did you become a knight?"

Sir Richard leaned back and tented his fingers. "Ah, I used to flatter myself that it was my cleverness that did it. But considering my run of failed experiments, I'm beginning to believe it was only dumb luck."

Henry stayed silent.

"Six years ago," Sir Richard continued, "I was in my study at Oxford. Out of sheer boredom, I twisted a thin piece of metal between my fingers and stared at the heap of parchments I was supposed to be reading. Then it occurred to me that I could twist the metal into a particular shape to hold all those parchments together. It wouldn't help me read them any faster, but at least the pile would be neat. And so, the parchment clip was born. I was hailed as a great inventor and knighted. I've been trying to invent something else ever since."

"Well," Henry said, "you invented a giant tarantula."

"True, but I don't know how I did it and, in any case, the real goal is to invent something that benefits mankind and does not require being chased into a forest with a torch."

Henry lay in his bed, mulling over what Sir Richard had said about Mary staying in the Queen's Forest. It made sense. There was plenty of game in the woods, so she would not have to come out because she was hungry. As long as she didn't stumble out of the woods in front of anybody, she should not cause any problems. Could she be counted on to do that, though? After all, she was Mary, Queen of Scots—reckless, daring, and adventurous.

He rolled over and stared at the leaded glass windows that kept the damp outside. It was pleasant to consider what the weather might be out of doors, now that he no longer had to live in it. Henry had spent months sleeping in London doorways, shaking in the cold and swatting flies in the heat. The nights were terrible, but sometimes the days were less so. If it were warm, Henry would make his way down to the harbor, where the breeze off the water was cool, and watch the ships sail in. It always struck him that the boats were attached to nothing, until the crew dropped a mighty anchor. That's what he felt he had done at the manor. Dropped his anchor.

The smoldering embers in the bed warmer sent heat through Henry's toes. As he stretched them out, he got that familiar sinking feeling. No matter how good anything got, there were his toes to think about. All six of them on both feet. His mother had told him they were the devil's work. She said he would get hanged if anybody saw them.

Henry pulled the blanket up to his chin. He had to stop thinking about his toes. Nobody ever wanted to look at another person's feet anyway.

# CHAPTER FOUR

A pounding on the front doors woke Henry. He staggered out of bed. Sir Richard did not employ a footman; it was Henry's job to answer the door to callers. They hadn't had any callers since he arrived, so he had not done it before. He buttoned up his waistcoat and ran down the stairs.

The councilman, Mr. Snidefellow, stood tapping his cane on the stone steps. Henry thought he was a "too" sort of person. Too tall, too thin, too bony, too pinched in the face, and too scowling.

"Good morning, Mr. Snidefellow," Henry said.

Mr. Snidefellow looked down his too long and too thin nose.

There was something Henry was supposed to say to everyone who arrived at the manor, except if it were the duchess, who was to be shown in immediately if she did them the compliment of coming to call. She had not done so since Henry had arrived, but he had practiced the manner in which he would politely show her to her special chair and then run as fast as he could to tell Sir Richard and then fly to the kitchen to tell Mrs. Splunket to make tea. It was all to go off smooth and quick and he was always at the ready for the moment when she would arrive. He was less ready for anybody else and needed to think what Sir Richard had directed him to say.

It finally came to him. "Unfortunately," Henry said, "Sir Richard is engaged. Would you like to leave your card?"

Mr. Snidefellow rapped his cane on the top step. "Certainly not. Show me in. I will see Sir Richard this instant."

Sir Richard had not told Henry what to do if a caller demanded to see him that instant. And worse, it was Mr. Snidefellow. Henry was certain Sir Richard did not want to see Snidefellow at any instant.

"Sir, I'm not sure I can—"

"Show me in, boy. I'm a busy man."

Henry knew Sir Richard wouldn't like it, but how was he to refuse? He did not dare cross a councilman.

"Well?" Snidefellow said. "As you appear not to know what to do next I shall tell you, direct me to the drawing room."

"There, sir," Henry said, pointing to the front room that was meant for visitors.

Mr. Snidefellow narrowed his eyes at Henry, then he strode into the caller's drawing room.

Henry thought he had probably not made a very good impression, as he had forgotten that he was meant to lead a caller into the room, not point at it and follow behind. He would have to be more careful next time.

Mr. Snidefellow perched himself on the yellow brocade upholstered chair. The very chair that Sir Richard had told Henry about. He had no choice but to say something.

"Excuse me, sir," Henry said. "I only mention this because I've been given strict instructions about it. That chair is only for the duchess."

"The duchess and I are great friends," Mr. Snidefellow said. "She will be delighted to discover that I have had the use of her chair. You, being a mere boy raised in the depraved alleys of London, could not comprehend the delicate feeling between two highly cultured people. Do not even attempt it."

Henry supposed he had Bertram to thank for being called "a mere boy raised in the depraved alleys of London."

As Henry turned to go and give Sir Richard the bad news about who was calling, Mr. Snidefellow said, "I note that there is no butler in the house. I will assume that although your upbringing has not exceeded the standards of a common pirate, you will know enough to at least alert the housekeeper that a distinguished guest has arrived and direct her to fetch tea."

Now he was a common pirate? He really would have to figure out what to do about Bertram. Henry said, "Yes, sir," but decided Mrs. Splunket would be happier not knowing about the distinguished guest.

Henry ran up the stairs to Sir Richard's bedchamber. Sir

**49**

Richard was just buttoning up his coat when Henry told him that Mr. Snidefellow waited to see him in the caller's drawing room.

"He's in the house?" Sir Richard asked.

"Yes, sir," Henry said.

"That is unfortunate. He's come to call on me before, but until this moment he's never set a foot indoors. Mrs. Splunket has always been very good about peeking out the window, seeing it was him, and hiding out in her nook until he left."

"I should have peeked out the window too, but I didn't and he was very forceful."

"Blast it," Sir Richard said. "I've managed to avoid the man quite successfully so far. The day after the tarantula's run at cucumber sandwiches is a most inconvenient time to have to receive him. There must be something we can say to make him go away."

"He seemed very determined, sir."

Sir Richard suggested various reasons why he couldn't see Mr. Snidefellow, ranging from having cholera to being out of town. Finally, convinced that the councilman would not be put off, he said, "All right, I'll see what the man has to say. If he stays too long, I will claim I am coming down with scurvy and must excuse myself to go eat a lime."

"But, sir," Henry said, "didn't you say scurvy only happened to sailors and that's why they carry limes on the ship? Because the limes prevent the disease?"

"Indeed," Sir Richard said, finishing the last button, "but he won't know that, will he?"

Sir Richard entered the drawing room and stared at his guest. Snidefellow rose and bowed stiffly. "Sir," he said, in a way that made a person feel like he really said, "Scandalous rogue."

Sir Richard waved a dismissive hand and said, "Yes, Snidefellow, what is it?"

Mr. Snidefellow sat down and said, "I have had reports of an unusual event occurring at the duchess's dusk-to-dawn croquet party. As the croquet party is the event of the season in this county, I object to anything unusual happening at it and find I must investigate. I will not allow, sir, for the good lady's plans to be trifled with."

Sir Richard folded his arms. "Did Henry tell you that you're sitting on the good lady's chair?"

Mr. Snidefellow sprang to his feet and pursed his lips. "He mentioned it."

"The duchess is very particular about that chair. She picked out the fabric herself and I had it specially made in London. Absolutely nobody is to sit on that chair but the duchess herself."

"I did not come to discuss chairs, sir. The reports I have heard are disturbing."

"You weren't there, then? Not on the guest list?" Sir Richard said. Henry thought he looked a little smug.

Mr. Snidefellow fussed with his cravat. "The duchess—who is a great friend of mine—enjoys my company on a regular basis. She knows of my busy schedule and the serious engagements I am . . . engaged in. She would not burden me with such frivolities."

"Ah," Sir Richard said. "Nobody would ever accuse *you* of frivolity."

Mr. Snidefellow's face had taken on a shade of red. He was clearly not accustomed to being talked to in such a manner. "Sir Richard," he said, "I have come here to demand an explanation. Something unsavory went on last evening and I demand to know what it was. There were reports of an unearthly creature."

"An unearthly creature?" Sir Richard said, laughing. "What sort of unearthly creature?"

"That's what I'm here to find out!"

"All I observed was a very ordinary-looking wolf," Sir Richard said, lounging on a sofa and looking bored with the whole conversation.

"We do not have wolves in this part of England!" Mr. Snidefellow said.

"It appears we do now," Sir Richard said coolly.

Henry had been standing behind Sir Richard's sofa. A movement out the window caught his eye.

Behind the councilman's back, Mary lumbered out of the forest.

Henry tugged on Sir Richard's sleeve. "Sir," Henry said quietly, "I'll just go feed the horses. Especially Mary."

Sir Richard's head snapped up. Henry prayed that Snidefellow would not decide to turn around.

"Each to his own tastes," Mr. Snidefellow said, his eyes on Henry, "but if I employed a servant, I wouldn't allow him to interrupt a conversation between gentlemen."

Sir Richard ignored him and said, "Good idea, Henry. Just be careful. She bites, you know."

Henry raced from the room as Mr. Snidefellow expounded on how he also wouldn't allow a horse to bite him.

The kitchens were at the back of the manor, facing the forest. Henry was going to need Mrs. Splunket's help to lure Mary back into the forest. The problem was what to tell her. But then, for all he knew she had already seen the beast.

Mrs. Splunket was grinding dried herbs with a mortar and pestle. A large pork roast sat on the counter beside her.

"Mrs. Splunket," he said.

She turned around. "You gave me a start, dearie." She peered at him. "Now look at you, all aflutter. What's got you worked up?"

Henry took a deep breath and said, "I've got some bad news. About an experiment."

Mrs. Splunket narrowed her eyes. "Of course you do. When is there ever any good news about an experiment? Sir Richard hasn't gone and burned off his eyebrows again? I told him I won't stand for it. We were the laughingstock of the village last time."

"No, nothing like that. It's about the tarantula John Fitzwilliam gave him. She's now rather larger."

Mrs. Splunket sprang into the air and landed on the counter with a thud. "Lord love me, tell me that thing ain't loose in the house."

"She's not in the house, but I really need that pork roast. Do you mind if I take it?" Before Mrs. Splunket could say whether or not she minded her pork roast disappearing, Henry grabbed it and ran out to the kitchen garden.

"That roast is for dinner," Mrs. Splunket called after him. "Them piranhas are eating us out of house and home."

Henry thought he would have to somehow make it up to Mrs. Splunket as he weaved down the narrow kitchen garden paths. He dodged pots of herbs, a trellis of climbing beans, rows of cabbages, and raspberry bushes. As long as the tarantula didn't move herself directly in front of the kitchen window, Henry didn't think Mrs. Splunket would be able to see her. That would be for the best, since the housekeeper clearly didn't comprehend how *much* larger Mary had become, and it would be better if she never did.

Henry fumbled with the latch on the gate and burst onto the back lawn.

The stables stood to the left of the narrow stretch of green that separated the estate from the Queen's Forest. On the right side, the piranha pond with its mermaid fountain sprayed water into the air and a gazebo lined with benches sat close by the house.

The tarantula swayed next to the pond and lowered her large head to the water. She suddenly reared back.

Piranhas had latched onto one of her pedipalps, the short appendages near the creature's mouth. Three of the silvery six-inch-long fish flapped back and forth, seeming determined to hold on to their prey, though they could not survive out of the water for long.

Mary knocked her pedipalps against the side of the pond and shook the piranhas free. One by one, the fish disappeared into the water with a splash.

Henry skirted the lawn and dashed toward the forest. At the tree line, he softly called, "Mary, look!" He waved the roast over his head.

The spider turned from the fountain. She paused and lifted her front legs, as if she were sniffing the air with them. Then she lumbered toward Henry and the forest.

He waited until the creature got within twenty feet, threw the pork roast into the trees, and ran. Henry paused near the gate to the kitchen garden. Mary charged into the forest after the roast. Henry supposed she had not yet learned to hunt larger prey and was hungry.

Henry ran through the kitchen. He apologized to Mrs.

Splunket about the roast, but didn't slow down to hear what she would say about it. He would pick her a bouquet of the nicest flowers he could find and make her a heartfelt apology after Snidefellow left the house.

When he returned to the drawing room, where Mr. Snidefellow and Sir Richard were still in conversation, Sir Richard glanced at him. Henry nodded.

Mr. Snidefellow paced the room, his arms clasped behind his back. "It is not unknown that our queen will acknowledge when a mistake has been made in bestowing a knighthood. Just three years ago, that swindler Boswellan was stripped of the honor. I do feel, good sir, that if my questions are not answered, I may have to recommend the same in your case."

Sir Richard rose from the sofa and stared directly into Snidefellow's eyes until the councilman was forced to look away. "Mr. Snidefellow," he said, "you are not welcome to interrogate me. As for making recommendations to our queen, I doubt you would be asked to recommend the time of day to Her Majesty. I am quite sure you have never been through the doors of St. James Palace and never will. Good morning." Sir Richard slightly nodded his head. As he turned on his heel and strode from the room, he said to Henry, "Show him out."

Henry suppressed a smile. When Sir Richard decided to put on his knightly airs, he was pretty impressive.

Mr. Snidefellow called after Sir Richard, "The duchess is the queen's cousin and has great influence. The duchess trusts my advice implicitly. I am not without connections."

Sir Richard waved a hand over his head in response before disappearing down the hall.

Mr. Snidefellow turned to Henry. "Boy," he said, "I want to know what occurred last evening."

Henry was silent. He had not expected that the councilman would interrogate him. He had the urge to run and get as far away from Snidefellow as he could. If he were in London, he would now be flying down an alley.

"Answer me, boy."

Henry composed himself. He wasn't a vagrant in London anymore. He was under the protection of Sir Richard Blackstone and he should start acting like it. He was pretty sure that men like Snidefellow could smell fear. "Sir Richard said that you're not allowed to interrogate," he said in as firm a manner as he could muster.

"Sir Richard has claimed I cannot interrogate *him*, and he shall find he is mistaken. He said nothing about you."

"But he would have meant me, too," Henry said. "We do almost everything together."

Mr. Snidefellow folded his arms. "I'm sure you do. Sir Richard has always been suspect in my mind. This isn't the first time I have been forced to wonder what sort of degenerate activity is carried out here. But what I find interesting is that this devil's work should increase so dramatically upon *your* arrival. Very interesting, indeed."

The devil's work. Henry glanced down at his feet. Could the man see right through the leather of his boots?

Mr. Snidefellow pulled on his gloves and slapped his hat on his head. "I'll be watching, boy. Watching closely." He stomped out of the room and the front door slammed.

Henry stood in the middle of the drawing room, thinking about what Snidefellow had said. They had better do something about that tarantula. A councilman was not one to fool with. Sir Richard might look at him as an annoying nuisance, but Snidefellow had power. And, if he wasn't lying about it, he had the duchess's ear as well.

As Henry thought to go find flowers for Mrs. Splunket, a pounding sounded on the door.

The man was back? What should he do? Sir Richard would not want to see him again under any circumstances. Maybe he should just pretend he didn't hear the knock? Nobody could get in trouble for not answering their front door if they hadn't even heard it.

The pounding sounded again. Henry tiptoed to the window to peek out. Just as he neared the glass, a boy's face suddenly appeared on the other side. Henry jumped back, and then looked again. The boy made a face at him. Henry made a face back, sticking out his tongue. Then he noticed that the boy was dressed in blue and white livery.

He was a footman to the duchess! Henry had practiced so many times what to do if she came and there she was, left to stand outside like a traveling tinker while he was making faces at her footman.

Henry raced to the front door and swung it open. "My deepest apologies, Your Grace!"

Rather than finding the duchess, the footman was alone. He was a tall boy, but appeared to have grown too fast for his body to keep up; he was all knees and elbows and sharp cheekbones.

"Her Grace ain't here," the footman said, smirking. "Billy Brash is here, known to the duchess as William as she don't like nicknames. Her Grace asks that Sir Richard attend her."

"Very well," Henry answered, relieved he had not insulted the duchess by leaving her outside. "What day shall he come?"

"Today," Billy said.

"All right," Henry said, "what time?"

"Now. She's a duchess, you rube. She don't wait for nobody."

Before Henry could protest that he was not a rube, the footman punched Henry in the arm. He turned and jogged back down the lane, laughing until Henry could hear him no more.

The duchess wanted to see Sir Richard now. That was not a good sign. It sounded less like an invitation and more like a summons. She was sure to want an explanation about her wrecked croquet party. Sir Richard might refuse to tell Snidefellow anything except that the disruption was caused by a wolf, but the duchess might demand more of an explanation than that.

# Chapter Five

Sir Richard marched up the duchess's drive. Henry jogged to keep up with him. It was a blustery day and the wind bent the top branches of the old oaks that lined the lane. Sir Richard held his hat on, and his coattails flapped behind him.

"Have you thought of what you will say?" Henry asked, breathless.

"As little as possible," Sir Richard said. "When in doubt, say as little as possible."

The duchess's estate was three stories tall and comprised of two massive wings joined at the center by an oval-shaped structure. All was done in limestone and there was a matching barn of equal grandeur to the left of the main house. Formal gardens were laid out to the right of the house. Henry figured there must be at least one hundred and fifty rooms to such a place.

Before Sir Richard had a chance to pull the doorknocker, the doors swung open. Croydon, the old butler, stood ramrod straight, staring over Sir Richard's head. In a rumbling voice, he said, "Her Grace, the Duchess of St. John, awaits you in the drawing room. This way, sir."

Henry followed Sir Richard inside. The oval in the center of the building contained a great hall, with various rooms on either side. He marveled at the twenty-foot ceilings, the glittering chandeliers, and the polished marble floors. The mahogany walls were lined with gold-framed portraits of dukes and duchesses, their children, their dogs, and their horses.

Sir Richard entered the drawing room, while Henry waited in the great hall. The butler had been called away by the housekeeper. Henry suspected he was meant to go to the kitchens to wait, as he had no business lounging around in this part of the house, but he decided he'd rather hear what was said.

He peeked around the doorframe. The drawing room furniture was all painted white and upholstered in pale blue silk. Draperies ran floor to ceiling over the windows and were done in cream brocade. A light-colored Persian rug covered the floor. A white porcelain teapot decorated with tiny red roses sat on a table next to a delicate matching cup and saucer. It was so different from Sir Richard's sparse furnishings of dark wood. Henry hoped Sir Richard wouldn't spill his tea or break the cup if the duchess served it to him.

The duchess herself was far younger than Henry expected. He had assumed she would be an old dragon, but she looked to be just in her late twenties. She wore a simple blue velvet gown and her wavy blond hair was pulled up atop her head and secured with a diamond clip. She nodded slightly. "Sir Richard."

Sir Richard bowed.

"You know why I have asked you here, so speak," the lady said, arranging the folds of her skirt around her.

"I am at your service," Sir Richard said, then stood silent.

Henry supposed this was what Sir Richard had meant by saying as little as possible.

The duchess sipped her tea and set the cup down. "As you are well aware, my annual dusk-to-dawn croquet party was a disaster. One of my footmen remains abed, under the impression that he saw a demon and is going mad. Rumors are flying about the county. What I observed with my own eyes was you and a boy galloping around on horseback, waving torches as if *you* were the madmen. Did you purposefully set out to ruin my party?"

"Certainly not," Sir Richard said.

"I wonder," the duchess said. "You've not made it a secret that you find the pastime beneath your notice."

"I never did say that," Sir Richard said.

"Perhaps not outright, but as you never attend that is your opinion spoken quite plainly."

Sir Richard took a step forward. In a low voice, he said, "Now, Darla, don't be—"

"Pardon me?" she asked in a cold tone.

Henry cringed. He thought Sir Richard had made a mistake in calling her by her Christian name. She did not seem surprised by it, just annoyed, so he supposed Sir Richard had done so in the past. Now, however, when she seemed so aggravated, it would probably be better not to take any liberties.

Sir Richard retreated. "Your Grace," he said, correcting himself.

"Mr. Snidefellow believes something evil is afoot here," the duchess said. "He has just been to see me and does not countenance your claim that you chased off a wolf. I myself find that hard to believe. Fortunately for you, Mr. Snidefellow always thinks something evil is afoot. So, I shall not take his counsel to request my cousin the queen relieve you of your knighthood. But mark me, Sir Richard, if anything like this happens again—I will."

Sir Richard bowed, and said, "I understand, Your Grace."

The duchess looked away from him and said, "That is all."

Henry turned to bolt back to the front door. He ran straight into Billy Brash, who had snuck up behind him.

"Ain't you the cad, spying at doorways," Billy said.

Henry froze. For all he knew, it might be treason to spy on a duchess. "Don't tell anyone," he whispered, hoping Billy Brash would take pity on him.

"Tell?" Billy said, looking highly insulted. "What do you take me for, a ratter?"

Henry had no idea what a ratter was, but guessed it was some kind of informant. "No, I didn't mean that," he said. "I just meant—"

"I know what you meant," Billy said, laughing. "You're a serious sort, ain't you? Get on with you," he said, punching him again in the arm and pushing him toward the door.

Henry was relieved that the footman wouldn't turn him in for a spy, but he began to think that his arm would get very sore if he saw much more of Billy Brash.

As Henry and Sir Richard walked down the lane, the wind blowing as hard as ever but this time at their backs, Sir Richard said, "That went better than expected."

"Did it, sir?" Henry asked, thinking that was not how he would have described what he had heard of the meeting.

"I thought you were listening at the door. Did you not think so?"

Henry colored. It seemed that everybody but the duchess knew he had been listening. "The duchess sounded plenty mad, sir."

"Yes, of course, she is furious," Sir Richard said. "But she's furious that we were galloping around waving torches. Not because we were galloping around waving torches at a giant tarantula. See the difference?"

Henry did see the difference, and he supposed it was good news that the duchess had not actually seen Mary. She had sounded so angry that Henry could not imagine what she would have been like if she knew a giant tarantula was the cause of the uproar.

"We'll think of a way to make it up to her. Buy her some pretty little porcelain thing. That's bound to do the trick."

"Would something like that impress the duchess?" Henry asked, skeptical. "If you really want to make it up to her, she'll probably want to know that you put some real effort and thought into it to show how sorry you are."

Sir Richard laughed. "You are right. Darla—I mean the duchess—is rather special. We must do better than porcelain."

"What about a puppy?" Henry asked. "Farmer Giles has a litter of spaniels just turned eight weeks. I saw them myself last week when you sent me to get bacon for Mrs. Splunket."

"A puppy? That's a capital idea. Was it a good-looking litter?"

Henry did not know what a good-looking litter might look like. "I suppose so," he said, "they were all brown and white and seemed friendly enough."

They reached the end of the duchess's drive and turned left, heading down the lane to Giles Farm. They passed Blackstone Manor and continued on until they were just a quarter mile from the post road. The wind had begun to die down and they strolled leisurely down the shady road.

As they discussed how long it might be before Sir Richard was back in the duchess's good graces, Henry said, "She was awfully upset over just a party. I could understand if it was a wedding, but those swells were only playing croquet in the dark."

"Yes," Sir Richard said, "but she's got her reasons."

Henry looked at Sir Richard expectantly.

"I shall acquaint you with her history, as it was told to me by Mrs. Splunket when I arrived," Sir Richard said. "It is well known in these parts so I tell no tales, but on no account ever speak of it if the duchess is nearby."

Henry crossed his heart, though he hardly thought it was necessary. If the duchess were nearby, Henry would not dare say anything at all.

"Mrs. Splunket tells me that the duchess was once Ms. Darla Kensington," Sir Richard said. "At just seventeen, she married the duke. For several years the duke and duchess lived contentedly enough. However, one circumstance blighted their happiness. They were childless. After three years they had quite given up on the idea of a family. But just as they had resigned themselves to it, a son came along."

Henry had never heard of a son, or a husband either. As far as he knew, she lived all alone in that rambling estate with only her staff. "Was it a fever or a pox that took her family?" he asked.

"Neither," Sir Richard said. "The duke was slain with a dagger. The boy disappeared."

"What?" Henry asked. He wondered why Mrs. Splunket had not told him that there had been a murder right next door.

"When the baby was just a year old, he was taken by kidnappers. A ransom note was received, with a meeting place in a cave that lies just beyond the post road. The duke insisted he go alone to drop off the ransom and retrieve his son, just as the note had directed. Little is understood of what occurred in that lonely place, but it was clear there was a struggle. The duke was killed and the boy never returned.

"So now," Sir Richard continued, "the duchess clings to her parties and you must not fault her for it. She has had an unhappy life, but finds solace in surrounding herself with gay faces."

Sir Richard stopped at the well-traveled lane that led to Giles Farm. "Here we are."

It was a short walk to the farmhouse, and a noisy one, too. The moment they stepped onto Giles Farm, barks erupted from all directions. The farmhouse, small and rugged and made of stone and thatch, was just ahead.

Farmer Giles, alerted by his spaniels, strode out of the cottage. He was a rough and weathered old man. Henry nodded to him, having already found out that Giles was not a chatty individual. Sir Richard fumbled around, searching for some subject that would engage the stone-faced farmer.

"You have a fine farm here," he said.

Farmer Giles glanced around at it and said nothing.

**67**

"I hope we find your family in good health?" Sir Richard said.

"My wife has the rheumatism," the farmer answered.

"I heard your dogs as I came in," Sir Richard said.

"Most folk do," the farmer said, "unless they be deaf."

Finally, Sir Richard said, "I understand you have developed your own breeding techniques." Giles's face lit up and they spent the next hour discussing canine genetics while Henry played with the puppies.

The puppies were kept in a stall, having recently been weaned from their mother. There were six altogether, spread out on fresh hay. Five were solid little beings, round and fat and bounding around on sturdy legs. One, small and thin, hung back with a shy and fearful look. Henry had not even noticed that one when he had first seen the puppies and wondered if she had been hiding. He wore out the bigger pups with play and laughed as he watched them fall asleep—fighting the urge until they could fight no more and collapsed where they stood. He edged over to the small one, which sat watchfully in the corner of the horse stall.

"There now," he said softly, "come here." He gently picked the puppy up. The undersized spaniel sat on his lap, staring at him with round brown eyes. Though she was small, Henry thought she was the prettiest of the litter, being mostly white with brown ears.

Giles and Sir Richard leaned over the stall door, negotiating the sale. "It is the duchess, after all," Sir Richard said. "It

**68**

really must be the pick of the litter. As much as you don't like to give him up, if the duchess were to own one of your line, every man in the county would know that Giles understands a thing or two about breeding spaniels."

"What about her, sir?" Henry said, holding the small puppy up.

"That's the runt, Henry," Sir Richard said. "Do you want me to be in even more trouble with the duchess than I already am?"

"But what if nobody wants her, just because she's small?" Henry said.

Farmer Giles rubbed his grizzled cheek and said, "Don' worry 'bout that. If the little thing don't gain weight in the next week, I'll snap her neck. Be a kindness, as she won't be no use to nobody at that size."

Henry leapt to his feet, clutching the puppy to his chest. "Kill her?" He turned to Sir Richard. "Could I have her, sir? I could use all my wages to buy her. I'll find her food . . . I'll even eat less myself . . . you'll not even know she's around . . . look—she's as quiet as a mouse!"

Sir Richard sighed. "I am not opposed to a dog around the manor. But the runt?"

"Please, sir." Henry's heart had begun to beat hard in his chest. He couldn't bear to imagine the little dog being killed.

"You understand she might not even survive?" Sir Richard said. "Many of the small ones don't."

Henry did know that. He had known of smaller children

dying on the streets of London. Their frail bodies couldn't hold up against the heat, cold, and hunger of living out of doors. One day you saw them on your usual route through the city, the next day you didn't.

"I understand," Henry said firmly.

Farmer Giles was amused by the idea that somebody wanted to buy the runt of the litter. He joked that a dog like that wouldn't grow big enough to win a fight with a cat. Seeing Henry's grieved expression, he softened and said, "There now, there's no accountin' for taste. Take her for nothing; I was just going to snap her neck anyhow."

Henry carried his puppy in his arms as they walked back to the manor. He named her Matilda and was greatly relieved to have arrived at Farmer Giles's farm in time to save her from having her neck snapped. He held her under his coat so she would not become chilled in the wind, though it had dissipated to a soft and gentle breeze. Still, he felt he couldn't be too careful as his puppy had a rough start in life. She would need a lot of attention to prove Farmer Giles wrong about her.

Matilda seemed to sense that she had just taken a great step up in the world and by turns looked eagerly about at the countryside and at Henry with a loyal gaze.

It was arranged with Farmer Giles that the pick of the litter, a hefty male, would be delivered to the duchess that very afternoon. Farmer Giles would hand it over to the butler with a message that it was compliments of Sir Richard.

As they turned down the lane toward Blackstone Manor, Henry squinted his eyes at the edge of the forest. Thin strands of white hung over tree branches and draped down to the ground like so many sewing threads. "Sir, just there. Is that—"

"Spider silk," Sir Richard said, nodding his head. "As it appears we cannot count on the Theraphosa nigrum lapis to remain hidden in the forest, I'd better spend the rest of the day in the laboratory searching for an antidote."

Henry thought of questioning the prudence of that. Sir Richard's experiments only went in two directions—nowhere or wrong—but the knight had such a determined look on his face that Henry decided to stay silent. In any case, he had a puppy to look after.

Mrs. Splunket took one look at Matilda and fell deeply in love. Henry's notion that he would have to scrounge up food for his new charge quickly fell by the wayside. Mrs. Splunket rummaged through the kitchen stores and tempted the puppy with every tidbit she could think of.

"Will you look at that appetite," Mrs. Splunket said, feeding Matilda a bit of toast with butter. She leaned down and cupped the puppy's face in her hands. "From now on," she said, "I'll see to it that you can eat as much as you can fit inside of you. To thank me for my trouble, you're to guard this place and keep out the vermin. In particular, any large spiders you may see creepin' about."

Henry felt bad that Mrs. Splunket was under the illusion that Mary was small enough to be conquered by an under-sized puppy. On the other hand, he reasoned, would it really help her to know the truth? She'd probably have nightmares. He'd already had a few himself.

Henry left Matilda under the supervision of Mrs. Splunket and ran to the stables to find Bertram. He had the idea that there might be some old horse blankets lying around the barn that would make for a cozy bed. He hoped he would not find the coachman in too bad a mood.

"Bertram," he called.

"If you want to ride your horse, you know how to saddle him," Bertram called from his hay bales. "Don't expect me to be doin' everything for you; I ain't your manservant."

"No, I don't want to ride," Henry said, thinking he pretty much never wanted to ride Cantankerous if he could help it. "I was wondering if you have any old horse blankets I can have."

There was silence for a moment, then Bertram said, "I see. So you find yourself a bit chilly in the manor, do ya? I suppose it ain't never occurred to you to wonder how a coachman is feeling. Is he cold at night? You wouldn't know because you ain't never asked."

Henry had come around to the stall that Bertram used as his daytime bedchamber. The coachman was lying on a bale of hay and chewing a stalk of it. "Are you cold at night in your cottage?" Henry asked.

"I ain't, but this is the first you know about it. As it happens, I'm as cozy as a bug in a rug in my little house. The point is, you didn't know. I coulda frozen to death and you'd be none the wiser."

Henry sighed. Since it was early spring, he didn't think it very likely that anyone would freeze, even if they were sleeping outside. "I don't want the blankets for myself. I've got a puppy and I want to make her a bed."

Bertram sat up on his hay bale. "A puppy? Here? What kind?"

"She's a spaniel, only if you're anything like Farmer Giles, you should know that she's the runt and that I don't care a bit about it. She's the best dog in the world and I won't have a word said against her."

"Who's sayin' anything against her?" Bertram rubbed his chin. "Well, if I'm to give up some horse blankets, it seems right that I should be introduced to them that's takin' 'em."

"Oh. You want to meet her?" Henry asked. He was surprised to hear that, but pleased. Bertram's mood seemed to have brightened considerably at the news of a puppy in the house.

"Seems to me that would be proper procedure," Bertram said. "Where is she?"

Bertram sat on the floor of the kitchen and held Matilda in his arms. "She's a good-looking dog," he said. "Don't you mind that she's on the small side now. Mrs. Splunket will fix that. I was on the small side myself before being exposed to her cookin'. No, this here dog reminds me of a dog I had in my youth. Juno, she was called. She was as loyal as they come and this one ain't no different."

Henry glanced at Mrs. Splunket. She shrugged her shoulders. He would never have guessed that a puppy would be the way to cranky old Bertram's heart. Maybe now the coachman would stop describing Henry as a common pirate to everybody he met.

Bertram made Matilda a bed out of every horse blanket he could pull out of the barn, excepting only the ones that were actually on a horse, and put it next to the kitchen fire. Henry had explained to Bertram that he planned to keep Matilda in his own room at night so she wouldn't feel lonely or afraid, but he also wanted her to have somewhere warm and comfortable to sleep during the day.

"Exactly as it should be," Bertram said, nodding in approval. "Now for myself, I'll just stop by in the daytime to see how she's getting on. You'll want someone experienced with dogs to consult with over her progress."

The puppy, stuffed with food and her stomach round and firm, looked at her three admirers and then waddled over to the pile of horse blankets and fell asleep.

A cry from the laboratory broke the friendly silence. "What the devil!" Sir Richard shouted.

Mrs. Splunket snorted. "There he goes again, another experiment down the drain."

Henry raced down the corridor. Sir Richard jogged around the laboratory, chased by a housefly the size of a pigeon. The insect landed on his desk and used its large front legs to wash its face. Its mirror-like eyes shined green and blue.

"Sir," Henry whispered. "How?"

"Edge toward the windows, Henry," Sir Richard said. "Get them open."

Henry moved slowly so as not to startle the creature. It had a nervous, fidgety look. He slowly turned the latch on the first window and pushed it open. The fly had not moved from the desk. He opened the rest of the windows, one by one.

"Come around by me," Sir Richard said.

Henry edged along the walls to the opposite side of the laboratory.

"Now, all we have to do is spook the creature toward an open window." Sir Richard grabbed a sheaf of parchment and waved it at the fly. "Shoo!" he cried.

The fly shuddered, then took flight off the desk and buzzed around the room. It knocked into a wall, then found an opening and flew out into the front garden.

Henry and Sir Richard raced to the windows. The fly attempted to land on a leaf of an old oak tree, but the leaf collapsed under its weight. It fell to the ground and struggled to right itself.

Sir Richard rapidly closed the windows.

The fly got itself airborne again, flew over the tops of the trees of the Queen's Forest and disappeared.

Sir Richard sank down in a chair. "Well," he said, "that's done."

"But, sir, how did it happen?"

"I wish I knew. As there is nothing to be done about Mary until we find a method of shrinking her size, I was looking about for some creature it might be safe to experiment on in hopes of discovering an antidote. All I could find was that Musca domestica, and I was lucky I did, as the sundew catches nearly everything that wanders in. A common housefly may not be very exotic, but serviceable all the same. As we can see, my antidote was not a success. Well, chin up I suppose. I could always—"

"Sir," Henry said, interrupting Sir Richard. "Who is that?" He pointed at a man striding up the drive.

Sir Richard peered out the window. "Good grief. It's Mr. Craven, Snidefellow's assistant. Get rid of him. Tell him I died very suddenly from an infectious disease and he must

**76**

go away immediately if he wants to avoid catching it. It would not do for that fly to circle back around and land on the man's head."

Henry ran to the door and opened it. He decided he had better disregard Sir Richard's instruction that the knight wasn't available because he had unexpectedly died. "Good afternoon, Mr. Craven. Sir Richard is engaged at the moment. Would you care to leave your card?" Henry said.

"No need," he said. "No need at all." Mr. Craven removed a parchment from his waistcoat and unrolled it with a flourish. He placed spectacles on his nose and read:

> *Sir Richard Blackstone is hereby summoned to a meeting of the village council tomorrow at six o'clock in the evening to answer questions regarding the circumstances and events on the night of the Duchess of St. John's annual dusk-to-dawn croquet party. Sir Richard is made to understand that this is not a request, it is an official summons.*

# CHAPTER SIX

After Snidefellow's assistant left, Sir Richard took the summons from Henry and tossed it into the fire. "That rascal will get more than he bargained for by summoning *me*," he muttered. "I have a mind to invent something that would sew a councilman's lips together."

Henry and Sir Richard spent the rest of the day in the laboratory, attempting to determine which ingredient was the culprit that had caused both the tarantula and the fly to assume massive proportions.

Late that afternoon, Sir Richard held his head in his hands. "The only common ingredient in both experiments is the dried powder from the leaves of the Amazonian lupuna tree, but that makes no sense. I've got the description of it right here." Sir Richard held up John Fitzwilliam's journal, filled with his friend's close and neat writing. He read the entry aloud:

*The lupuna tree is feared by the natives, as they believe the tree can wreak vengeance on unlucky souls*

*who offend it. For myself, I find it has profound medic-*
*inal qualities. I became quite ill with fever during a*
*jungle sojourn some weeks ago. When I could walk no*
*farther, I rested against one of these mighty trees. My*
*native guide warned me against it. I tried to reason*
*some sense into the man and then amused myself by*
*quoting a bit of Garibaldi's ode to nature: 'Mother*
*Earth and Brother Tree, I love thee well, watch over*
*me.' As the night progressed, I experienced a terrible*
*thirst and gratefully drank the water collected on the*
*tree's leaves. I was cured by the following morning.*

*I have harvested some leaves, dried them, and*
*ground them to a powder. On my return to England I*
*will deliver them to my old friend Blackstone to study.*
*Whatever is at work here appears to counter weakness*
*and restore strength and vigor. Of course, my native*
*man is now convinced that I made some sort of magic*
*and his people have been repeating the ode to nature*
*ever since. It amuses me no end that the worst poet in*
*England has now got devotees in South America.*

Sir Richard laid down the parchment. "You see, Henry,
I used the powder on the Theraphosa nigrum lapis to extend
her life, then I used it again on the Musca domestica while
attempting an antidote. I would believe that somehow an
unusual effect had been produced by an unwanted synergy
with another ingredient, but there is no other ingredient used
twice in these two experiments. It's got to be the lupuna tree

that is causing this mischief. There's something about it that Fitzwilliam did not discover."

Henry pondered how the lupuna tree powder might have taken a wrong turn until he was called away from the laboratory to answer the door.

He had not seen who had come up the drive, so he peered out the window first. It was Billy, looking as brash as ever.

Henry swung the door open and said, "Does the duchess want to see Sir Richard again?"

Billy shrugged and said, "I doubt it; she's too busy feedin' the best bits of meat to that dog. She sent this," he said, handing over a sealed parchment. "It's probably about that dog. Everything in the whole household is now about that dog. Speakin' a dogs, I heard you got one too. Can I see it?"

"Why?" Henry asked. He felt very protective of Matilda and would not want her to be insulted by anything Billy Brash might have to say about her size.

"To play with her," the footman said. "Nobody has got a chance to play with the duchess's dog—he ain't been out of her sight."

Henry considered this, then he said, "I'll have you know that my dog is smaller than the duchess's dog. On purpose. If you can swear not to comment on her size, then you can go around back and ask Mrs. Splunket to let you into the kitchen. I will warn you, though, Mrs. Splunket will throw you out on your ear if you say one word against Matilda."

"Not a word against her," Billy said, crossing his heart.

The footman made to punch his arm, but Henry saw it coming and dodged. He punched Billy instead and slammed the door shut.

Henry ran back to the laboratory and delivered the note from the duchess to Sir Richard.

Listen to this," Sir Richard said.

*Sir Richard—*

*I should be very cross with you right now. Of all the underhanded tricks, you send me a puppy with soulful brown eyes, and the temperament of an angel, and a particular penchant for sitting on my lap. Alas, you have weakened my defenses in the most devious way. I have named him Harold and we are already great friends.*

*Fondly,*

*Darla*

"Well!" Sir Richard said. "She seems very pleased. Excellent idea, Henry. Most excellent."

Henry took Matilda out on the front lawn before going to bed. She nosed around in the grass and made a run at a passing moth. Suddenly, her tiny body went rigid. A low growl erupted from her throat.

A black shadow lumbered along the edge of the forest. Henry scooped Matilda into his arms, ran inside and bolted the door.

The following evening, the carriage rumbled through Barton Commons' only road to the church at the far end. Sir Richard had determined to take the carriage to the council meeting, even though the village of Barton Commons was within easy walking distance. He said that arriving in state, like the knight that he was, would put a pause in some of the council members' minds. Then he said, "And of course, we wouldn't want to meet Mary on the road."

The church was made of local stone and topped by a tall steeple. The village council meetings were always held there, as it was the only building large enough to hold more than ten people, aside from The Buck and Boar Tavern across the road, which was deemed a less appropriate place for serious council business.

Henry peered out the window. There were a few farmers' carts, but Sir Richard's was the only carriage in sight. The duchess had not come. He had half-hoped she would, as she was so happy with her puppy that Henry thought she would be kindly disposed toward Sir Richard. Henry did not think anybody else in Barton Commons had any influence over Mr. Snidefellow.

Bertram opened the door. Sir Richard hopped down and said, "We shan't be long." He jogged up the stone steps of the church, threw the doors open, and strode inside.

The council sat in a row of chairs set up on the altar. Mr. Snidefellow sat in the middle, with Mr. Craven on his right and the magistrate, Mr. Neville, on his left. The quiet and retiring curate, Mr. Small, stood next to Mr. Neville with an uncomfortable look on his face.

Curious villagers and men who rented the duchess's outlying farms filled the forward pews, except for the very first row, which was reserved for local gentry. Sir Richard nodded and smiled at the crowd, and even winked at a woman who had obviously worn her best Sunday cap for the proceedings. The matron blushed and the two young girls next to her giggled into their handkerchiefs.

Sir Richard gave the council a slight bow. Henry slid into a pew.

"Well?" Sir Richard asked in a booming voice. "Here I am. What is it you want?"

Mr. Snidefellow cleared his throat and said, "Sir Richard, I attempted to gather information from you about the cause of the disturbance on the night of the duchess's dusk-to-dawn croquet party. As you have shown yourself to be uncooperative, you have been called before the council to be questioned formally."

"What is your question?" Sir Richard asked tersely.

Mr. Snidefellow waved to Mr. Small and said, "Proceed."

Mr. Small blushed. The gaunt curate shuffled forward with a look of apology to Sir Richard. "Sir," he said in a trembling voice, "very sorry to trouble you. Mr. Snidefellow was just wondering if you could provide some illumination as to what caused the fright that evening." Mr. Small then nodded his head up and down vigorously, as if Sir Richard had already answered the question to everyone's complete satisfaction.

"It appeared to be a wolf," Sir Richard said.

Mr. Snidefellow motioned for Mr. Small to step back. The curate looked relieved and hurried away. Mr. Snidefellow rose. "Sir Richard, you know very well we have no wolves in these parts. You were seen riding about on horseback, with that urchin you brought from London, waving torches at some kind of creature."

Sir Richard crossed his arms and said, "The boy has a name: it is Henry Hewitt. We were indeed out riding that evening. When we heard a commotion erupting from the duchess's lawn, we immediately rode to the scene and grabbed the torches to better see what was the matter. Of what I could observe in the shadows, it appeared to be a wolf."

Mr. Snidefellow pursed his lips and said, in a loud voice sure to reach all of the villagers' ears, "We shall not harbor the devil's intrigues in this blessed hamlet of Barton Commons. I know my duty and, as councilman, I will not sit by while farmers lose their stock, fields fail to produce, fruit withers on the vine, and our innocent babes are carried off. Those are the consequences of allowing Satan to take up residence."

"Satan?" Sir Richard said. "Have you lost your wits entirely?"

The curate looked as astonished as Sir Richard and boldy spoke up. "My dear sir, there can be no cause for talking of the devil! The church would wish to make every effort to discover some rational explanation."

"There is every reason to talk of the devil," Mr. Snidefellow said.

Sir Richard laughed, but as Henry looked around, he could see that Mr. Snidefellow had made an impression. As much as the church dismissed talk of the devil being the cause of blight and disease, many people still had a habit of looking in that direction when any sort of bad luck befell them. Henry could see that Snidefellow was determined to exploit their fears and superstitions.

Snidefellow continued. "I have reason to believe you know something of the devil," he said to Sir Richard. "Is it not true that the very year you arrived, our fields were blighted? And is it not true that just last year, Widow Darylrumple's cow died in mysterious circumstances?"

"What's any of that got to do with me?" Sir Richard asked.

"Of course you will claim it is coincidence," Mr. Snidefellow said. "Satan loves to hide behind such things. But

I would also point out that it appears the evil is intensifying, and it has coincided with the arrival of that boy."

Snidefellow pointed to Henry, who sank in his seat, silently repeating to himself, *Don't say my toes, don't say my toes.*

"There is something strange about the arrival of that boy," Mr. Snidefellow said, glaring at Henry. "A dozen boys in this village might have been hired as your assistant, but you thought it necessary to hire a street urchin from London. I am certain you have brought him here to assist you with your dark purposes. Who better than a boy who has not been taught morals, who has lived on the streets, no doubt engaging in every sort of crime, who has no nearby family he might be guided by or confide in?"

Snidefellow turned away from Henry to Sir Richard. "It was no wolf out that night. It was a padfoot."

"A padfoot?" a woman cried from the back of the church.

"A black dog, straight from hell. I don't yet know what sort of rituals you have conducted to loose such a creature upon these innocent people, but I intend to find out. I will conduct a full investigation."

The magistrate, who was a dull man and a great friend of Mr. Snidefellow, nodded his head in approval.

"Take your devil's assistant and leave this hamlet forever, or face a trial and a hanging once I have uncovered the truth," Mr. Snidefellow said.

Sir Richard smiled. "So that's it? You want me to pack up and go?" Sir Richard turned to the villagers, who were now huddled in the pews. "You have heard what your councilman has to say. Now hear me. Neither I, nor my assistant Henry Hewitt, have anything to do with the devil. The padfoot is an old wives' tale. What Mr. Snidefellow's motive is in these ridiculous accusations, I do not know, other than to be certain that he has some vile motive. If you need further assurance that talk of a padfoot is ridiculous, talk to your curate and hear your own church's opinion on the matter."

A man threw open the doors to the church, interrupting Sir Richard. It was Croydon, the duchess's butler.

Henry smiled. So the duchess knew about the council meeting after all, and had sent her butler with a message.

"The duchess's spaniel," Croydon announced in his usual formal tone, "answering to the name of Harold, has gone missing this very night. The duchess offers a ten-pound reward to the individual who safely returns him."

The church erupted. "Ten pounds! For a dog! But who's willin' to go out into the night with a padfoot about the place? No, thankee, I'd rather stay poor and alive."

Sir Richard glanced at Henry. They both thought the same thing. It was no padfoot that took the puppy. It was Mary.

Sir Richard addressed Mr. Snidefellow. "You have said what you wanted to say, as have I. Now, I warn you that if you continue this harassment, there will be consequences. Step lightly if you know what's good for you."

He leaned down and whispered to Henry, "Get to the carriage."

Bertram held the door open and said, "Home, sir?"

"No," Sir Richard said. "But stay here a moment."

Henry jumped into the carriage after Sir Richard. He shut the door behind him and said, "Sir, where would Mary take poor Harold?"

Sir Richard rubbed his chin. "I cannot be certain. From observing her behavior in the aquarium, we know she likes to wander, but she prefers a secure spot to retreat to. Especially when she has prey. I imagine size has not affected her instincts."

"We'll never find her if she's gone deep into the Queen's Forest."

"True. And she may well have, but only if she were able to discover some likely den to hide herself. I have not seen such a place in my wanderings. She also keeps making appearances, and so I must guess she has not ventured overly far into the wood."

"Maybe she got into one of the farmers' barns?" Henry asked.

"Possibly, though I think any sort of livestock in the barn would sound the alarm. I know Real Beauty would kick her stall door down if she were to see such a beast. Cows and sheep could be expected to be equally alarmed, and a farmer is rarely out of earshot of his herds."

"The cave perhaps?" Henry asked. "The one where the duke met the kidnappers? You did say it was an out of the way and lonely place where he was killed."

Sir Richard took a moment to consider. Then he said, "Yes, indeed. If the creature has found the cave, she would like the environment. I have been there myself from time to time, looking for interesting flora and fauna. I have never been inside, but the opening is certainly big enough to admit her. It is lonely and secluded, another point in its favor."

Sir Richard opened his door, leaned out, and said to Bertram, "Take us beyond the manor, pass Giles Farm, and stop just beyond the post road."

Sir Richard closed the door. "I only hope we get there in time."

"Will she wrap the puppy in her web?" Henry asked.

"That evidence of silk we saw near the road was not the beginnings of a web. She was nearby and had left the strings of silk to alert her to anyone approaching. No, what she will do is release poison through her fangs, and then slowly inject digestive enzymes until . . ."

"Until what?"

"Until Harold is liquefied from the inside out."

The jostling carriage and the idea of Harold getting liquefied made Henry's stomach flip-flop. He had a sudden urge to run home and make sure that Matilda was safe, but he reminded himself that Mrs. Splunket would be sitting in front of the kitchen fire with his dog. Mrs. Splunket would never let anything happen to Matilda.

The carriage barreled past the lights of lonely farmhouses, candles in the windows flickering orange and yellow. Henry's mind kept drifting back to Snidefellow's talk of the devil. Did it mean that the man would always be on the lookout for any signs? Did the councilman know that six toes were said to be a sign? Henry shivered at the idea that the councilman might line up everyone in the village and demand to see their feet.

The carriage trotted past the post road. To the left were fields of wheat, to the right a steep, wooded slope rose. Bertram reined in the horses.

Sir Richard jumped down from the carriage and handed out swords from the compartment on the back. He passed one up to Bertram.

"Keep your wits about you and guard the horses," Sir Richard said.

Bertram held the sword in front of him like it was a live snake. "Guard the horses from what?"

Sir Richard did not answer, but strode up the slope leading to the cave.

Henry heard Bertram mutter, "Highwaymen, I suppose. Though why we're out in the dark looking for trouble when any sensible person is at home with a puppy, I'll never know."

The slope took them ten feet above the road and then

leveled out to a flat grassy area. It looked like a small plateau, as the slope then continued upward for another hundred feet. Sir Richard motioned for Henry to stop. A gaping hole of darkness showed on the side of the incline. The entrance to the cave. Henry shivered at the thought of the duke climbing to the very spot they stood upon, in hopes of retrieving his son, and having no idea that he was getting ever nearer to his own murder.

"Devil take it," Sir Richard whispered, "we forgot torches."

Just then, the clouds over the moon cleared off and the scene became brighter. It was easier to see the landscape, but Henry did not think that would help once they entered the cave.

A bright sparkle nested in the grass caught his eye. "Look, sir," he said. A small collar lay on the ground near the entrance to the cave. Sir Richard scooped it up and held it in front of him.

It was made of leather and encrusted with pale blue stones that glittered in the moonlight. "This has to belong to Harold," Sir Richard said. "Only the duchess could afford to put jewelry on a dog."

Henry examined the collar. The leather had been cut clean through. "I'm afraid we may be too late."

"Perhaps," Sir Richard said. "But we've got to be sure."

They crept closer. Henry heard a faint whimper.

"He's in there!" he said, bounding toward the entrance.

Sir Richard grabbed Henry by the back of his coat. "Yes, and he's alive. But the spider will be in there too. We must go carefully."

# CHAPTER SEVEN

They cautiously stepped inside the entrance. Henry felt his way along the right side of the cave while Sir Richard took the left.

The cave was dank, its walls slimy and wet. It smelled of decaying leaves, as if cleansing sunshine had never penetrated its darkness.

The whimper came again. It was on Henry's side and he fell to his knees. His hands touched a soft and slightly sticky substance that seemed to cover the cave floor.

"Stay where you are," Sir Richard whispered from the opposite side of the cave. "I will make my way over to you."

Despite Sir Richard's directive, Henry crawled toward the sound of the frightened dog.

A lump lay just in front of him in the gloom. He lunged toward it. It was Harold. Henry swept him up in his arms.

"I have him!" he called to Sir Richard.

Henry turned to run as a massive leg swung toward him. He dodged the tarantula. As he reached Sir Richard at the entrance, Henry heard a whooshing sound. Stings radiated across Henry's back as if he had been stabbed by a hundred sewing needles.

Sir Richard grabbed the puppy from Henry's arms, and they scrambled down the hill. Bertram stood on his seat, waving his sword at the darkness. Sir Richard swung the carriage door open. "Bertram," he cried, "to the manor as fast as you can!"

In the darkness of the carriage, Henry perched on the edge of his seat. He did not want to push the barbs deeper into his back. He used one hand to hold on to the window frame to steady himself. Bertram was driving the coach like a demon—shouting at the horses and using his crop. Henry guessed poor Bertram thought they were being pursued by highwaymen.

Henry was determined to say nothing of the barbs in his back. Once Harold was taken care of, he would see if Mrs. Splunket could get them out. He could tell her they were . . . he didn't know what he would tell her they were. Maybe he could say he fell on some kind of spiky plant.

Harold lay on Sir Richard's lap, looking dazed and weak. Henry knew from observing Matilda that a puppy did not like to stay in one place. She was always getting distracted and going one way and then, just as fast, going another. The fact that Harold was so still and did not try to wriggle out of Sir Richard's arms was not a good sign.

"Have we got him out soon enough?" Henry whispered.

Sir Richard peered down at the weakened puppy. "Only time will tell. I'll treat him as best I can and we'll see how he goes. He has been poisoned, no doubt of that. With any luck, it has not been too much and he may be able to overcome it. He does not move much, but he has not been entirely paralyzed, and that is a good sign."

They barreled down the lane toward the manor. In the dark of the carriage, Henry listened to Harold's labored breathing and tried to ignore his own flaming back.

At the front doors, Sir Richard leapt down with the puppy in his arms and raced inside. Henry slowly edged himself down to the ground.

Bertram had descended from his perch and prepared to unhitch the horses. "I don't suppose it's too late to have a look in on Matilda," he said.

Henry nodded and climbed the stone steps. As he passed by the torches that lit the portico, Bertram cried, "What's that sticking out of your back?"

Henry waved him on but did not answer.

He staggered into the manor. Sir Richard was already in his laboratory, shouting for Mrs. Splunket to build up the fire and bring blankets and warmed goat's milk. Mrs. Splunket hurried by Henry, then she stopped short. She peered at his face and said, "Dearie, you're white as a sheet. What's happened?"

Henry slowly turned to show her his back.

Mrs. Splunket shrieked. "For the love of heaven, what is that?"

"That's what I want to know," Bertram said, coming in behind Henry.

Sir Richard ran out into the corridor. "Henry! Why didn't you tell me you were hit?"

"Hit with what?" Mrs. Splunket cried.

"I'm all right," Henry said. "Take care of Harold." His voice sounded distant, as if he had left it down near the post road.

"Blast it," Sir Richard said, "the boy's about to faint."

Henry woke on a sofa in the laboratory. He lay on his stomach and his back stung as if he had rolled in a nettle patch. He cautiously reached around to feel for the barbs, but they were gone. A bright fire burned high, warming the room. On the floor next to him, Harold lay curled tight on a pile of blankets. Matilda lay next to the sick puppy, occasionally giving his ear a lick for good measure.

"Ah," Sir Richard said. "You are awake." He held a tray in front of Henry. Five barbs, each a half-foot long, were lined up in a row. "Just as well that Bertram and I removed them while you were out cold," he said. "We had to dig them out. I'm sorry to say you'll have some scars from it."

Henry wiggled his toes, then sighed with relief. Nobody had removed his shoes while he was unconscious. His secret was safe.

Mrs. Splunket bustled in, seeming recovered from her recent shock. "I see the patient is awake," she said brightly. "Sir Richard, I will take it from here. I've already set Bertram up with a generous cup of brandy and I suggest you sip the same." She helped Henry sit up and held a bowl of bone broth to his lips. "There now, we'll build up your strength in no time. Who'd have thought these devil highwaymen are out there inventin' new weapons? I never saw the likes of them," she said, glancing at the barbs on the tray.

Sir Richard cleared his throat and said, "Yes, indeed. The criminal element never rests."

"The puppy?" Henry asked, peering down at Harold. "Will he live?"

Harold had woken from the noise and stretched out. Matilda snuggled next to him.

"I believe so. He is weak, no question. But he was strong to begin, so I think we might be confident in his recovery. Matilda instinctively knows to keep him warm by staying near him, which is kindhearted of her. She was the runt and so would have been picked on and bullied by the other puppies, including Harold. If he is alive by morning, he can thank Matilda for it, and I daresay we could tell the duchess he has been found."

"'Tis just a shame that a person who would need an

extra ten pounds of reward money didn't stumble across him," Mrs. Splunket noted.

"Ah, but that's exactly how it was," Sir Richard said. "It was Henry, not I, who found the rascal. Harold would have succumbed to the elements if Henry hadn't spotted him lying at the base of tree."

Mrs. Splunket looked pleased. Henry was stunned. Ten pounds? His wages were only six pounds a year. "But, sir—"

"Nonsense, Henry. We won't say another word about it," Sir Richard said in a firm tone.

Mrs. Splunket gave Henry something bitter to drink that eased the pain in his back. It had a dreamy effect on him, and he lay with one arm hanging down, scratching Matilda's ears. He fell in and out of dozes as Mrs. Splunket crept in every hour, wrapped in an oversized blue robe, her hair up in curl papers. As the sky lightened to gray, it occurred to Henry that now that they knew where Mary had taken up residence, it would be easier to do something about her. While he was thinking about what it was they should do, he fell into a deep sleep.

The sun shone brightly through the windows when Henry woke. Matilda and Harold were tugging blankets between them, each battling for dominance with defiant puppy growls.

Sir Richard sat at his desk, shuffling papers. "Look, sir," Henry said. "Harold is playing. He's going to be all right."

"No doubt of it," Sir Richard said. "One of the remarkable things about a puppy, Henry, is they appear to have a memory like a sieve. I doubt Harold remembers a thing about his recent adventure. While you or I might be traumatized by such an event, Harold is living for *this* morning and *this* game and is not at all reflecting on what happened yesterday."

"Have you sent a message to the duchess to give her the news?"

"I thought we might take him back in person," Sir Richard said. "Assuming you feel up to it?"

"Yes, sir," Henry said, struggling into a sitting position. The fact was, he did feel better after a good sleep, though the skin that had been punctured by the barbs was sore and had started to itch.

The sun was high in a cloudless sky and the air was mild. Sir Richard carried Harold, as Henry had to keep scratching his back to keep the itching at bay. They happily strolled up the duchess's drive, both anticipating how pleased she would be to get Harold back.

Henry had resolved that he would not take the duchess's reward. He and Sir Richard had caused the problem in the first place and giving her a puppy had been Henry's idea.

Taking the money felt not exactly . . . on the up and up, as Mr. Clemens used to say.

The front windows of the duchess's estate were thrown open to admit the fine air of the day. As they neared the steps to the front door, they heard the unmistakable voice of Mr. Snidefellow.

"Your Grace," he said, in the sniveling tone he reserved for the duchess, "you must also consider your duty to the estate. You are still of . . . of," Snidefellow paused. "Well, you can still have children."

Henry and Sir Richard stared at each other.

"I already have a child," the duchess answered. "He will inherit the estate and carry on the line."

"Of course," Snidefellow said. "There is every hope the boy will be recovered. But in good conscience it would be wise to plan for, well in the unfortunate case that . . ." In a louder, more confident voice, Mr. Snidefellow said, "I have consulted this situation often in my prayers. God would wish you to remarry. To a moral man. A man who can be trusted to know the Lord's will."

Henry could not believe it. Was Snidefellow attempting to court the duchess? How could he ever think such a fine lady would marry him?

Sir Richard looked dumbstruck. Henry tugged on his sleeve and pointed to Harold. Sir Richard recovered himself and nodded. He rapped on the front door and waited for the butler to answer. Considering how prompt Croydon usually was about opening it, Henry suspected the butler had been at the drawing room door listening to Snidefellow.

Croydon saw the puppy. His face lit up and he chucked Harold under the chin. "There you are, you naughty thing!" He caught himself and put his stern butler face back on. "Normally, sir, I would not presume to interrupt the duchess while she is in conference with the councilman, but I believe I may make an exception in this case. Do go in."

Henry turned to wait outside, but Sir Richard put a hand on his shoulder. "You must come in, Henry. You rescued Harold, after all." He handed the puppy to Henry.

Henry flushed. He'd really rather wait outside, but Sir Richard strode forward and threw open the double doors to the drawing room.

Sir Richard stopped short. Mr. Snidefellow was on one knee in front of the duchess, who was studiously looking away from him.

"What the devil!" Sir Richard exclaimed.

Snidefellow struggled to his feet. Crimson crept from the top of his neckcloth to his hairline. "Sir," he said, "what is the meaning of bursting in here without even being announced?"

Henry hurried in and stood next to Sir Richard.

"Harold!" the duchess cried. "You've found him!"

The duchess ran to Henry and swept the puppy from his arms. Harold licked her face and his tail thumped against her gown. She whispered to the puppy as she sat down on a divan.

"Where have you been, you wayward little man?" She looked to Sir Richard and said, "Where on earth did you find him?"

Sir Richard bowed and said, "We searched for him last night and Henry spotted him at the base of a tree near the post road. He was in a bad way, so we nursed him through the night. As you can see, he has rallied nicely."

Snidefellow stood rooted to his spot. The duchess seemed to forget he was there. She nuzzled Harold and said, "Naughty you!" She held him up. "Has he sustained any serious injury? My goodness, look, right there on his neck, two puncture marks. Perhaps we truly do have wolves in the area."

"Just whatever poor Harold's adventures were, I cannot say, but I suspect he is lucky to have come through them," Sir Richard said.

The duchess rose from the divan and approached Henry. "You have restored a great happiness to me. I promised ten pounds to Harold's rescuer and so you shall have it."

"Please, Your Grace," Henry stammered. "I'd rather not."

"Rather not?" she asked. "Rather not have ten pounds?"

"Rather not," Henry repeated. "It was just by chance I found him. Anyone who was looking for him might have found him."

"Indeed," the duchess said. "However, I suspect not everyone was looking for Harold. *You* were."

"Well, it just does not seem to warrant a reward. Perhaps you could give it to the poor?" Henry said.

The duchess looked at Henry thoughtfully. Quietly she said, "As you wish." She turned to Sir Richard and said, "You have found yourself a little gentleman in this one."

Sir Richard bowed in reply.

"You must stay to lunch, Sir Richard," the duchess said.

"An honor," he said.

The duchess glanced over at Snidefellow, seeming to suddenly remember he was there. He had changed color from a blushing red to a sickly white. "Mr. Snidefellow, thank you for your call. Good morning to you," she said firmly.

Snidefellow had no recourse but to stiffly bow and leave. Henry thought he looked murderous.

Sir Richard and the duchess had a picnic in the gazebo in her back garden. Henry sat at the kitchen window with a plate of cold mutton and fried potatoes that the cook had kindly given him.

Sir Richard leaned toward the duchess and said something. The duchess threw her head back and laughed. Harold bounded around the gazebo, chasing his tail and enjoying the sunshine. Henry thought the duchess and Sir Richard looked natural together. They were a fork and a spoon, just like Mrs. Splunket said. And to think! Snidefellow had been down on one knee! Would she marry him? It seemed so farfetched.

The elegant duchess and the sneering councilman? But Henry had seen at the council meeting what a powerful persuader Snidefellow could be.

Billy Brash flew into the kitchen and was scolded by the cook. Considering how unconcerned he looked, Henry guessed that he always ran into the kitchen and she always scolded him for it. But she didn't seem to really mind. The footman threw himself into a chair. "I saw your dog," he said to Henry.

Henry knit his brows together. He was fully prepared to go toe to toe with the footman if there were any insults hurled at Matilda.

"I like her," Billy said.

"Oh," Henry answered.

"She's got a certain way about her," Billy continued. "A bit more refined than Harold, though I'd deny it if you told the duchess I said so."

"She *does* have a certain way about her," Henry said, warming to the subject. "I knew it as soon as I saw her. Did you know that Farmer Giles was going to snap her neck? I got there just in time."

"What?" Billy cried. "That woulda been a crime."

Henry and Billy spent the next hour comfortably discussing the merits of his dog. It was decided that Henry would apprise Mrs. Splunket of Billy's new standing as an admirer of Matilda, and Billy was to be let in to play with the pup at any time that Mrs. Splunket found convenient.

After lunch, Henry and Sir Richard strolled down the lane toward the manor. "All's well that ends well," Sir Richard said.

"Has it all ended well, sir?" Henry asked.

Sir Richard stopped in the lane and turned to Henry. "Don't you think so? Harold is back with the duchess and she's as pleased as punch about it."

"That part is good. But it seems like other parts aren't so good. Snidefellow was in a fury when he left."

Sir Richard waved his hand.

"And he was proposing, sir."

"The duchess will never marry a scoundrel such as that," Sir Richard said.

"Mightn't she not, sir? After all, he can be persuasive."

Sir Richard's lips compressed into a tight white line. "Darla, with that no-good, morally bankrupt windbag of a poser!"

Henry thought he could guess what was happening. Sir Richard was in love with the duchess, or very nearly so, but did not know it himself. It was exactly as Mrs. Splunket had believed. No wonder Sir Richard had made a special chair for her. Henry had thought that was odd, but had reasoned that it might be something you needed to do if you wanted a duchess to come to your house. Now he thought otherwise. "Mightn't *you* marry her?" Henry asked.

"I? Well, I certainly could—what I mean to say is, I have

**105**

considered from time to time, someday in future, right time and all that . . ." Sir Richard stopped speaking and stared into the distance.

"Perhaps, sir," Henry said quietly, "the right time is now. Before she marries Snidefellow."

"Now?" Sir Richard paced the lane, mumbling to himself. "It would be very sudden; she'd not see it coming. After all, I didn't see it coming. Still, Snidefellow! But now? Perhaps strike while the iron is hot? Don't overthink the matter. Yes. I'll do it!"

Sir Richard spun on his heel and strode back toward the duchess's estate.

# CHAPTER EIGHT

Sir Richard leapt up the duchess's steps two at a time and bounded through the front door without knocking.

Henry lingered on the steps after Sir Richard had disappeared inside. Now that he had suggested Sir Richard propose, he began to wonder what would happen to him if the duchess accepted. Would she let Sir Richard go on with his experiments? Henry didn't know the duchess very well, but it seemed like the kind of thing she wouldn't approve of. If she didn't like it and made him stop, Sir Richard wouldn't need an assistant anymore. What about Mrs. Splunket? Would she be out of a job too? Maybe he should have just kept quiet. The baker had always said, "If you stick your nose in another's business, don't be surprised if it gets chopped off."

Croydon poked his head out the door and looked about. Henry said, "Sir Richard's gone in. Best not interrupt him."

The butler had a puzzled look on his face, then he seemed to get Henry's meaning. "Indeed." He smiled and closed the door.

Henry paced outside the front of the house for more than an hour. Billy briefly hung himself out of a second floor window and called, "Why is he back?"

Henry explained, in no uncertain terms, that he was not at liberty to say.

Billy shrugged and shut the window.

Finally, Sir Richard burst out the front door.

"It's all settled," Sir Richard said. "She's agreed to it. Goodness me, I'm to be married!"

That night over dinner, Sir Richard said, "It turns out, she wondered why it took me so long to get around to asking. I explained I was merely waiting for the right time. She said, if all men waited for the right time, the human race would have died out long ago. I daresay she's right about that.

"I told her you were in the habit of dining with me and there were some sticking points there," Sir Richard continued. "She is a duchess after all, but she saw it my way in the end. You helped your case by not taking the reward; she thinks you have the instincts of a gentleman."

Henry was relieved that he would still have a job, but he was a little frightened of having to eat with the duchess. He didn't think his table manners would be up to her standards and if he knew anything about Billy, Henry guessed the footman would always be trying to make him laugh or drop something.

"Will Mrs. Splunket still be your cook?" Henry asked.

"Ah yes, it seems Darla's cook is planning to retire, so Mrs. Splunket shall continue her reign."

The rest of the evening passed with Sir Richard relaying more of his and the duchess's plans. The matrimonial banns would be read within the week.

Henry thought an unintended happy consequence of the engagement was that Snidefellow would likely drop his accusations against Sir Richard. As furious as the man would be to hear of the engagement, he would not dare go against the duchess. The councilman's living was hers to give and she could just as easily take it away. Henry doubted Snidefellow would be so rash as to risk his livelihood.

The next morning, Sir Richard wrote to John Fitzwilliam to invite him to act as best man, while Henry fed Mr. Terrible a handful of dead beetles. He had to be careful to drop them in without touching the sides of the aquarium in case there was any poison on the glass. A furious pounding on the door interrupted him.

Henry ran to answer it and found Farmer Giles leaning against the doorframe and out of breath.

"Oh no," Henry said. "Don't tell me Harold has run off again."

Sir Richard came out from the laboratory.

The farmer heaved in a breath and said, "A man's gone missing. Red Callahan. He was last seen leaving The Buck and Boar at eleven last night. We've searched the road from the tavern to his cottage, but there's no trace of him. He's a bad sort, and I'm guessing he came to a bad end, but he's a fellow human being so we've got to do our best to recover him."

"I know Red," Sir Richard said. "A terrible drunkard. He's probably sleeping it off in the woods."

"Aye," the farmer said. "But his wife is in a nervous state as this is the first time in her life that he ain't come home. The whole village has been out searching for him since early this morning. Not a trace of him to be found."

"We shall join the search willingly," Sir Richard said. "Though I suspect he'll make an appearance once he sobers up."

Farmer Giles seemed to have more to say, but kept staring at his shoes.

"What more?" Sir Richard asked.

"Ah," Farmer Giles said. "That councilman has been putting it about that it's a consequence of a padfoot bein' let loose on the neighborhood. First a dog goes missing, now a man. Next, it will be our children."

"That's preposterous!" Sir Richard exclaimed.

"I'm inclined to think so," Farmer Giles said, tugging on his cap. "But Snidefellow has been plantin' ideas in poor folks' heads. He says how comes it was you that knew where to find the duchess's puppy? He says you knew where the padfoot would take it, on account of it bein' *your* creature."

Henry gulped. Farmer Giles could have no way to know how close to the truth that really was.

Sir Richard said, "I'm glad you appear to have more sense than that. We shall set off at once and conduct a search for Red."

After Giles went away, Sir Richard said, "To the cave, quickly. And bring torches. If the spider has killed a man, we must dispose of the creature. And I must take full responsibility for the loss of life."

As they trotted toward the post road, Henry said, "What's a padfoot anyway? I never heard of it."

"Ah," Sir Richard said, waving his hand dismissively. "My old nurse told me the tale of the padfoot. She claimed it was a fierce-looking black dog with fire in its eyes—an omen of death. The beast moves silently, but one can detect its presence by the unusual tracks it leaves—six toes on both forelegs. My nurse used to claim it was always on the hunt for disobedient boys. Of course, a man of science does not give any credence to such nonsense. Though when I was a boy it was an effective deterrent to any trouble I might have thought up."

Henry gripped his reins in a tight fist. Six toes. It was too coincidental. Maybe his mother had been right—his toes really were a sign of the devil. Maybe he was turning into a padfoot in his sleep and then not remembering it in the morning. He would have to think of a way to find out. Of course, he had no idea what he would do about it if he were a padfoot. Was there some cure, or would he have to go away from people? Would he have to go and live somewhere deep in the Queen's Forest so that he wouldn't be a danger to anybody?

Henry and Sir Richard climbed up the slope to the cave. In the daylight, Henry saw that they stood on a flat ridge between the slope down to the road and a steeper slope up to the top of the mountain. The entrance to the cave sat as a black, open mouth looking to devour all who entered. The cheerful chirping of birds in the trees sounded unnatural near such a place.

"I don't hear a man," Sir Richard whispered. "Let us hope we are not too late."

Henry lit the torches from a flint and they stepped inside.

Now he could see the sticky material he had only felt on the night they had rescued Harold. Mary had spun a circular burrow inside the cave. It swept up the walls and covered the roof, creating an oblong nest. There was no sign of her. Or Red Callahan.

"Heaven help me if Darla ever saw this," Sir Richard muttered. "The very spot where the duke was killed, defiled by a creature of my own making."

They stepped carefully over the fine silk floor, some of it sticking to their boots. Henry was careful to keep his torch away from the walls, as the substance looked flammable. Strangely, as they went deeper into the cave it became lighter, not darker. Light shone in from the opposite end of the burrow. Henry had assumed the cave was sealed, but now he could see that it led somewhere else. Sir Richard and Henry crept toward the light.

The hole at the back of the cave was about six feet high and maybe seven feet across. The aperture overlooked a deep valley as large as a farmer's field. The bottom of the valley was flat, but its steep, grassy slopes rose up in sharp angles. Henry was certain there was no way in or out of the valley except through the cave. It looked as if no man had ever tread there. A tarantula had though.

Mary, Queen of Scots, sat at the opposite end of the valley, appearing at rest in the sunshine.

Sir Richard pulled Henry back into the darkness of the

cave. "There's no evidence of Red Callahan having been here. Until we can discover an antidote, we must block her escape. The other slopes are angled too steeply for her to climb. She's so top-heavy she'd tip over if she tried it. This is her only way out."

Henry nodded. They used their swords to cut through the nest material down to the earth below so they could reach the stones they would need to seal up the hole. They unearthed and began rolling stones from inside the cave toward the valley's entrance. It was grueling work, as the opening was large, but there were plenty of good-sized stones to do the job.

When they had piled rocks waist high, Sir Richard whispered, "By my life! Darla will want to see this."

Henry glanced over at him. Sir Richard was near a back corner of the cave and had pulled out his dagger. He carefully chipped around an area of dried earth.

"What is it, sir?"

"I've found a footprint from the boy. He must have stepped into the mud, poor thing. They didn't even put shoes on him."

Sir Richard dug deeper around the footprint. "There must be a good deal of clay in this soil—the imprint is hard and distinct."

Henry kept on, piling rock after rock. The wall grew so high that he had to stand on a second pile of rocks to reach high enough to set the stones.

Sir Richard deposited the earthen footprint into his satchel and returned to help Henry seal up the entrance. He hoisted Henry up to place the last stones.

Sir Richard set Henry down and they stepped back to view their handiwork.

"She'll never get through that," Henry said.

Henry and Sir Richard searched the surrounding woods for Red Callahan, or any sign of his liquefied body. The sun had passed over the noon hour, and the afternoon light, combined with a stiff breeze, sent shadows flying around the forest. Henry had usually found the forest welcoming in the daylight, but now that they searched for a man missing he felt it more ominous despite the sunshine. It was as if the forest transformed itself to meet a person's mood. That gave Henry the creeps and made him think of the sundew deciding to fold up its leaves around its victim. He did not like the idea that the greenery all around him could be thinking.

Late in the afternoon, Sir Richard sent Bertram to Farmer Giles with a message. They had found no trace of Red Callahan.

Sir Richard set off to see the duchess with his small clay footprint. He had told Henry that he would propose to cast it in plaster to preserve it.

Henry and Matilda stayed in the laboratory. Henry was

determined to discover an antidote for the tarantula. Mary was trapped in the valley at the back of the cave, but there was still a giant fly buzzing around somewhere. They could not afford to give Snidefellow any more reasons to accuse Sir Richard of the devil's work. The man might be cautious not to offend the duchess, but it occurred to Henry that Snidefellow was crafty and might attempt to stop the marriage in some underhanded way.

He pored over Fitzwilliam's journal and mapped out what had happened, step by step, when Fitzwilliam had come into contact with the lupuna tree. Fitzwilliam had been ill, then rested against the tree despite warnings that he should not do so, then he drank water collected on the leaves of the tree and was miraculously cured by morning. Had the water picked up some sort of property from the leaves? Or had it been something that rubbed off the bark of the tree? The tree had conferred strength to Fitzwilliam. Was it perhaps enough strength to cause the massive growth of Mary and the fly?

Henry eyed the lupuna powder sitting on a shelf above the aquariums. Did he dare try it on a plant?

The hairs prickled on the back of Henry's neck as he imagined the carnivorous sundew plant snaking its way along the lanes of Barton Commons, catching everyone in its wake and folding them up in its leaves.

No, he would keep the powder well away from the sundew. He would take it outside and try it on a small patch of grass at the edge of the Queen's Forest. That way, if the grass grew unusually high, it should just blend in with the trees and not be too noticeable. Hopefully.

Henry crossed the room and reached up for the bag of powder. He grazed it with his fingertips. The bag slipped off the shelf and Henry caught it, but not before a few specks of powder floated down on top of Mr. Terrible.

"Oh no," Henry whispered. He swept Matilda into his arms and ran out of the laboratory. He shut the door behind him and pressed his ear against it while Matilda licked his face. He had no idea what a giant poisonous frog would sound like, but all he heard was soft chirping. Henry jogged outside the manor and made his way to the laboratory windows. He peered inside.

Mr. Terrible was his same small size, but instead of sitting placidly on a rock as was his usual habit, he hopped madly around the aquarium. Henry squinted. The frog's tongue darted out and caught something small and brown. Then it caught another. The aquarium was filled with crickets.

Henry breathed a sigh of relief. He would not have to explain to Sir Richard that a giant poisonous frog now took up most of his laboratory. Henry paused. What had happened? Why wasn't he going to have to tell Sir Richard of the disaster? Why had the lupuna powder produced crickets instead of a giant frog? That made no sense at all. It was beginning to seem as if logic and the lupuna tree could not go together.

Sir Richard returned after sunset. The duchess had been overcome by the clay footprint and they had spent much time discussing the kidnapping. Sir Richard now knew far more than he had heard from Mrs. Splunket. The investigator, who remained on the case even now, was convinced it had been an inside job. The criminals had known when they would find the house empty, except for the nursemaid and the boy. The crime had taken place on May Day, and the staff had been given the day off to attend the festivities. The duke and duchess had been suddenly called to court, but when they arrived at St. James they found that no such summons had been issued. The poor nursemaid had been left to fend off three men. Their faces had been covered, so she could only describe them as two men tall and thin, and one short and stocky.

The duchess could not believe it was an inside job and was convinced that the culprits were highwaymen. It pained her to think so, for if the boy were still alive he was surely a thief by now. He would have no way to know his true identity and would only grow up to be whatever he had been taught to be. Sir Richard was determined to send the details of the case to his solicitor to see what else might be done.

Sir Richard leaned back in an easy chair and said, "And you, Henry. I see you've been poring over Fitzwilliam's journal. Have you discovered any clue I overlooked?"

"Not really," Henry said. "The lupuna powder is as mysterious as ever. I thought to try it on a plant, then I accidentally got some on Mr. Terrible."

Sir Richard sat up in alarm.

"But it didn't do anything to the frog. Instead, it filled his aquarium with crickets."

Sir Richard rubbed his chin. "That is most unexpected. But you say it was a very little amount of powder? Perhaps different amounts produce different effects? Well, no matter. Fitzwilliam will be here soon enough and we may question him in person. I had thought of writing to him regarding this . . . situation, but dared not, lest such a letter fall into the wrong hands. I have my suspicions that our good councilman examines the post."

"Did Red Callahan turn up?" Henry asked. He was not worried about Red falling victim to Mary, as she was safely trapped, but he did not like that so many people were searching everywhere for him. Somebody might go into the cave. They would be bound to notice the spider silk covering the walls and floor and the newly built wall at the back.

"No," Sir Richard said, "I met with Giles on the road. That confounded Callahan is still missing. We will set out early in the morning to continue our search for him in the Queen's Forest. I can't think where else the scoundrel could be."

That night, Henry had an idea on how he could make sure he was not a padfoot. He carefully wound a hair from Cantankerous's tail around the doorknob in his bedroom and then around a nail protruding from the wall. If he had been stalking the neighborhood in his slumbers, he would know it in the morning. The hair would be broken.

# CHAPTER NINE

Henry dreamed of walking past a looking glass and seeing a black dog with flaming red eyes growling back at him. He ran from the beast and it leapt out of the glass and gave chase. As fast as Henry ran, the creature was always just behind him, never catching him and never falling behind.

Soon after dawn, Henry woke, his sheets soaked with sweat. He scrambled out of bed. The horsehair he had tied across the door was intact. Whatever his six toes meant, at least he could be certain he was not a padfoot. He vowed not to think of it any further, as he was sure his nightmare of the beast had been caused by worry. He would rather not dream such a horror again.

Henry and Sir Richard rode in silence through the early morning, along the shady paths and sunny glens of the Queen's Forest. Deer darted away at their approach, crashing through the underbrush as they fled. Rabbit tails swished away under the greenery. Branches overhead rustled as birds took flight. Cantankerous took note of every movement, convinced that deer, rabbits, birds, speckled sunlight, and leaves swaying in the breeze were all equally dangerous. Henry wrestled to turn him as they picked up the main trail that led deep into the forest. It formed a long U shape, exiting at the opposite end of the village of Barton Commons, just behind the church.

Henry scanned in every direction for some clue, some shred of evidence, that Red Callahan had been in the forest—footprints, broken branches, a shred of clothing. He saw nothing.

The end of the trail was straight ahead. Bright sunlight shone just beyond the tree line.

"No luck here," Sir Richard said, breaking the silence. "We best track down Farmer Giles to determine where to search next."

Henry and Sir Richard trotted out of the forest.

A group of a dozen men stood in front of the church. Snidefellow was lecturing them on some subject. One of the men spotted Sir Richard and cried, "Look! He's right there!"

"What now?" Sir Richard muttered.

Mr. Snidefellow and two constables approached them. "Sir Richard," Snidefellow said in a loud voice, "you are hereby arrested for the murder of Red Callahan and the kidnapping of the duchess's son, William St. John."

Henry's thoughts spun off in a hundred directions.

Arrested? How could Snidefellow have the nerve to accuse Sir Richard of murder? Where had Red been found? What was the meaning of accusing Sir Richard of the kidnapping of the duchess's son? None of it made sense.

"What the devil?" Sir Richard said.

Snidefellow smiled. "You may well say what the devil, as that is exactly who you have employed in your nefarious work."

"What evidence have you?" Sir Richard questioned.

"That, you will hear at trial. Suffice to say, our esteemed magistrate has found the evidence compelling."

"That old magpie is your crony," Sir Richard said derisively.

"Ah! Now he denigrates the law! But of course, the devil knows no laws but his own."

"We should make a run for it, sir," Henry whispered. He felt sure they should get away. They should go somewhere away from the village to try to figure out what was happening. On no account should Sir Richard allow himself to be taken.

"No," Sir Richard said so that all could hear him. "A knight never retreats. I will face these ridiculous charges, and when I am cleared of them I will thrash this sniveling idiot to within an inch of his life."

Snidefellow colored. He turned to the men and said, "Hear that? He threatens to thrash a councilman? The very devil speaks out of his mouth."

"You're the devil," Henry cried, pointing at Snidefellow.

"Watch your tongue, you impudent urchin," Snidefellow said in a low voice, "or I'll have you taken in, too."

Sir Richard laid a hand on Henry's shoulder. "Tell the duchess what's happened, and Fitzwilliam as soon as he arrives. Write to my solicitor, Mr. Seamus Candlewick of Gray's Inn, and let him know he is wanted in Hampshire immediately."

Sir Richard dismounted his horse, handed Henry the reins, and submitted himself to the custody of the constables.

Henry struggled through the village atop Cantankerous and leading Real Beauty by her reins. He studiously avoided meeting anyone's eye. Like most villages, word of what had happened was traveling faster than he could ride. Mrs. Splunket had told him that people liked nothing so much as gossip. If a dairymaid spilled milk it would be known everywhere in the county before she had time to fetch her mop.

Henry left the village behind. As he made his way to the duchess's drive, a feeling of profound dread came over him. It wasn't just the idea of a private interview with the duchess, though that was bad enough. It wasn't just telling her of Sir Richard's arrest, though as they were recently engaged, that also was bad enough. It was *why* Sir Richard was arrested. A murder and a kidnapping. The kidnapping of her own son.

Where had they found Red Callahan's body? Had it been liquefied? Mary must have been out hunting on the night the man went missing. That would account for her sitting placidly in the sun in the valley beyond the cave the next day. She was full.

But the kidnapping? How could Snidefellow come up with any evidence that Sir Richard had anything to do with that? He did not even live in the county at the time.

Henry reached the duchess's door. Croydon took some convincing, but after Henry repeated three times that he had been sent with an urgent message from Sir Richard, and that it must be given to the duchess directly, the butler gave in. A groom led the horses away and Croydon showed Henry into the drawing room.

Henry stood waiting for the duchess. He tried to distract himself by examining a delicate porcelain figurine of a girl surrounded by flowers, but realized he might drop it if he weren't careful and quickly set it down. The more he tried to relax, the more he felt like his nerves were getting ready to explode inside of him. He concocted various ways to begin his speech, but each sounded worse than the next.

The duchess swept into the room. "What's this?" she asked. "What message do you bring?"

"Uh . . ."

"Well?" she said. "Out with it."

The duchess looked in a temper, and he had not even said anything yet. Henry took a deep breath and said, "Your Grace, I've just come from Sir Richard and—"

"Oh, I see," she said. "He's got cold feet, has he? And he's had the gall to send a boy to break it off before the banns are read?" The color rose in the duchess's cheeks. "Not courageous enough to do it himself, I suppose. He really has no claim to be a knight if he cannot even be bold enough to manage his own affairs."

The conversation had taken on a life of its own. How the duchess had arrived at the conclusion that Henry had come to break off the engagement, he had no idea.

"No," Henry said, "that's not it. Sir Richard is as much in love as ever."

The duchess did not look convinced.

"He's always talking about you and he's already invited his best man. Mrs. Splunket says Sir Richard has turned into a regular pile of mush."

The duchess sat down and composed herself, seeming pleased with this description of Sir Richard's state of mind. "Mush, you said? That will do. Very well, what is your message, young man?"

Now came the hard part. "Your Grace, Sir Richard has been arrested. By Mr. Snidefellow." Henry paused so the distressing news could really sink in.

The duchess laughed. "Is this some sort of jest?" she asked. "Am I to find that scallywag of a knight hiding behind the doorframe?"

Henry shook his head.

"Arrested?" she said. "Whatever for?"

Here it was. The worst news of all. Henry cleared his

throat and blurted out, "For the murder of Red Callahan and the kidnapping of your son."

The duchess was very still. "My son?" she said. "Tell me all. Everything you know. From the beginning."

Henry tried to tell her all, but he didn't know where Red Callahan's body had been found, or what condition the body had been in, or why Snidefellow would think Sir Richard was involved in the kidnapping.

"Did you know," the duchess said, "that Sir Richard brought me a footprint from my boy?"

Henry said that he did know about the footprint. He had been in the cave with Sir Richard, searching for Red Callahan, when it was discovered.

She pointed to a case that sat empty on a table. "I put it under glass, just there, to keep it safe until we had a cast made. Mr. Snidefellow came this morning and seemed quite shocked to see it. He insisted on taking it as evidence in the kidnapping case. I did not see how it could be particularly relevant. All it proves is that my son was in the cave, which we know because my late husband's body was found at that very spot. Still, Mr. Snidefellow was insistent and I thought he must see something in it that I did not."

The duchess paused, her hand resting on the glass case. "Could Mr. Snidefellow have possibly got the idea that Sir Richard was involved in the kidnapping simply for finding the footprint?"

Henry didn't answer, but he thought Mr. Snidefellow might have seen it as an opportunity and been glad to pretend that was what he thought.

"Though Mr. Snidefellow can be . . . misguided at times, I believe he is an honest man. Of course he is mistaken in this matter, his thinking has been led astray somehow."

"All I know," Henry said boldly, "is Sir Richard has not been involved in any crimes. He is the best person I have ever met. He's probably the best person in England."

The duchess smiled. "So say I," she said. "Now, the question is how to clear up this ridiculous misunderstanding. I'm surprised the councilman did not consult me before taking such a rash step. He did not even mention it this morning."

Henry was not as surprised as the duchess that Snidefellow hadn't mentioned it.

"We must not allow Sir Richard to linger in jail. This matter must be dealt with at once," she said.

Henry told the duchess that he would write to Sir Richard's solicitor in London, and that Fitzwilliam was expected to arrive any day.

"I shall write a note to Mr. Snidefellow and ask him to come to me," the duchess said. "He will see that he has made a mistake when I point it out to him."

When Henry left the duchess, he felt a good deal better than when he had arrived. She would make Snidefellow let Sir Richard out of jail.

Billy followed him to the stables. "What you been talkin' over with her Ladyship?" he asked.

Henry mounted Cantankerous. "I'm not at liberty to say. It's confidential business."

"Playin' it close to the vest, are you?"

"Very close, Billy."

The footman shrugged. "I been thinkin' we ought to give Matilda some kind of title, like she's real nobility. After all, she nearly got killed by Farmer Giles, and she lived to tell the tale. What do you say? I was thinkin' of Matilda, Queen of the Spaniels."

Henry did not at first answer. He thought it was an excellent idea, but he didn't want Billy to think that he could just go tacking names on to his dog whenever he felt like it. Finally, he said, "I will give that suggestion serious consideration."

Mrs. Splunket was outraged at the news of Sir Richard's imprisonment.

"The nerve of that rascal to arrest our good Sir Richard," Mrs. Splunket said, "whose only crime is that he is a very bad inventor."

Henry sat on the floor with Matilda. He had been nodding and agreeing with the housekeeper for over a half hour.

"The most my master is guilty of is burning off his own eyebrows and digging up my roses. I suppose one does not get arrested in England for ruining a garden?"

"Certainly not," Henry said, nodding.

"Well," she continued, "I will not sit idly by while the good man is sitting in jail. Who knows what sort of rancid food they might call dinner?" Mrs. Splunket proceeded to pack a basket of food. After she had packed enough for Sir Richard to live on for a month, she left for the magistrate's jail in the village to see that Sir Richard was cared for properly. Considering her red face and the pace at which she marched down the drive, Henry thought Mr. Snidefellow would be wise to stay out of her way.

Henry had just finished the letter to the solicitor when Mrs. Splunket returned. She dropped down into an overstuffed chair in the library and scooped Matilda onto her lap. "Well," she said, still out of breath from her walk, "I never heard of such a thing. Sir Richard is accused of murderin' a man that ain't even been found and kidnappin' a baby afore he ever set foot in the county."

"Wait," Henry said. "Red Callahan has not been found? But then, how do they know he's dead?"

"That's what I'd like to know. As they tell it in the village, the magistrate has gone and declared him dead, as he ain't been seen in two days. They reason that old Red was heavy on the drink, and as he hasn't been seen at The Buck and Boar, his liver couldn't stand up to a dryin' out and he must surely be dead somewhere. They say Snidefellow had it from a doctor that a man like Red would die of the delirium tremens if he don't make it to a tavern every day."

"That's ridiculous!" Henry cried.

"A course it is," Mrs. Splunket answered. "But that Snidefellow has got them poor souls to believe all manner of things. They ask me, how is it that Sir Richard found the puppy? And how is it that Sir Richard found that footprint from the boy when all those investigatin' that cave never did find it?"

"Because it was hidden behind a rock!" Henry said.

Mrs. Splunket looked puzzled. "What was you two doing looking for Red Callahan behind a rock?"

Henry gulped. He had not dared tell anybody about what had really happened to Mary but Mrs. Splunket's loyalty was unquestioned. And, he reasoned, she already knew the tarantula had gotten bigger. Just not how much bigger.

As Henry told her about the experiment gone wrong, Mrs. Splunket's face changed from wonder to shock, then to fury.

"That man!" she said. "I told him no good would come from those experiments. When creatures from the Amazon jungle started turnin' up, I said—there's no way a knowin' what goes on in those kind of wild places. Mary, Queen of Scots, indeed."

"Mr. Fitzwilliam should be arriving any day," Henry said, hoping to cheer her up. "Perhaps he can explain more about the lupuna tree."

"Lupuna tree," Mrs. Splunket said, her voice full of disgust. "Whoever heard of such a thing? Why did Sir Richard have to go messin' with foreign trees, I'd like to know? He shoulda kept his eyes on a good old oak. English trees don't do nothing unusual."

"We have to find Red Callahan," Henry said. "If we do that, Snidefellow's whole case falls apart."

"Aye," Mrs. Splunket said. "*If* that old devil Callahan is still alive. He ain't been seen one way or another."

The following day, Henry took Cantankerous down every deer path in the Queen's Forest that he could find. It was the first time he had ventured into the woods alone and he hoped it would be the last. He would not be anywhere near it if it weren't necessary to find Red to exonerate Sir Richard. Every snap of a branch or rustle of a leaf felt dangerous. There were times Henry worried he might get lost and not be able to find the main trail again. The forest was vast and it felt alive to Henry, as if it watched him and if he let down his guard it would trap him somehow. He kept reminding himself that could not be true and was just caused by his idea that the sundew must be able to think, but it did no good. As the sun began its slow descent and the shadows deepened, Henry hurried back to the stables. He was greatly relieved to be out of the forest but discouraged at his lack of progress. Red Callahan had disappeared without a trace.

That evening, Henry took Matilda out on the lawn. He had the uncomfortable feeling of being watched again, as if the forest had a hundred eyes upon him.

Henry was startled from his thoughts by the clip-clop of a horse's hooves on the drive. A rider had turned into the lane and galloped toward him. A tall, tanned man about thirty years old wheeled in his horse, jumped down from the saddle and said, "Fitzwilliam here. Tell your master I am at his service."

It took a good deal of time to acquaint John Fitzwilliam with the facts, such as Henry knew them.

They sat in front of a crackling fire in the library, long into the night.

"This is a fine state of affairs," said Fitzwilliam. "Here I am, ready to stand steady by his side at the altar, and the old boy has created a couple of creatures and got himself thrown in the clink for murder and kidnapping."

Henry thought that was one way to put it. He said, "We were anxiously awaiting your arrival to find out more about the lupuna tree."

"I'm afraid I don't know more than I wrote."

"Sir Richard is certain that the lupuna powder caused the . . . undesired effect," Henry said. "What's strange, though, is why the different effects? It cured you of your fever and it filled Mr. Terrible's aquarium full of crickets, yet it turned Mary, Queen of Scots, and the Musca domestica into giants."

"Wait, what?" Fitzwilliam said, putting down his glass of brandy. "Who is Mr. Terrible? Mary, Queen of Scots, died centuries ago."

"Oh, sorry," Henry said. He had become so used to the names he had forgotten that Fitzwilliam would not know anything about it. When Fitzwilliam had collected the specimens they only had their Latin names, not the names Henry later gave them. "Mr. Terrible is the Phyllobates terribilis. Mary, Queen of Scots, is the Theraphosa nigrum lapis. We call her Queen of the Scots because of her daring and impetuous nature."

"I see," Fitzwilliam said. "Blackstone wrote me to ask permission to name the species after himself, which I heartily gave as there is no Latin word for Fitzwilliam. But he failed to mention the Queen of the Scots being at all involved."

"I named her that," Henry admitted.

"I suppose it doesn't matter what you named her, as she's unlikely to come when called. All right, so why the different effects? Who knows? It *is* called the giant lupuna tree. I suppose that would account for the tarantula and the fly turning to giants."

Henry sat up straight in his chair. "Giant? That wasn't in your notes!"

"Wasn't it, though? I was sure I had described it as rather large."

"That could be a clue to why the powder had the effect it did," Henry said, "though it doesn't answer why the powder doesn't always turn things bigger."

"Well, as you say, the tarantula is safely trapped in the valley beyond the cave," Fitzwilliam said. "The fly has not reappeared, so I think we can safely assume it has become dinner for a hungry falcon. The real question is, how do we find out more about this Snidefellow character? The only way to help Sir Richard is to bring that scoundrel to his knees."

Fitzwilliam took a swig of brandy. "I need to find out more about that man," he said, "and, Henry, you're going to help me."

# Chapter Ten

The following morning, Fitzwilliam and Henry prepared to execute Fitzwilliam's daring plan. Fitzwilliam would waylay the warden, while Henry broke into Snidefellow's cottage and searched for any information that might help Sir Richard. Privately, Henry thought it was less like a plan and more like a way to join Sir Richard in jail. He argued that they should wait to hear the advice of Sir Richard's solicitor, but Fitzwilliam was resolute. They must act now.

Snidefellow's cottage was hard by the church and backed onto the Queen's Forest. Fitzwilliam would approach by the road that led through the middle of Barton Commons while Henry would come through the forest so as not to be observed.

Henry spurred Cantankerous through the woods. He turned onto the main trail that led deep into the forest. The hairs on the back of his neck stood up. Once again he felt watched. Mary was safely trapped in the valley, and he did not fear the fly. But perhaps there really were wolves nearby?

Or even a padfoot if such a thing existed? He could not rule that out entirely, as he had never known that a poisonous frog or a tarantula actually existed until he saw them with his own eyes. Though Henry reasoned with himself that there was nothing in the forest to be frightened of, his instincts kept telling him otherwise.

He decided that he couldn't entirely dismiss his feelings. His sense of impending danger had served him well on the streets of London. He had often had a sudden idea of something being not exactly right and then, when he looked about him, saw a pickpocket reaching for his cup or a constable giving him the eye or his parents coming around a corner. Henry did not know what could be causing him to feel such a deep sense of alarm now, but he decided to be extra watchful.

Cantankerous seemed to sense danger also and was unusually cooperative. The pony moved to a trot and did not once pause to bite at Henry's leg. Finally, Henry saw the light at the tree line that marked the edge of the Queen's Forest.

He silently dismounted, tied the reins to a sturdy tree limb, and crept to the back of Snidefellow's cottage. After ten minutes of waiting, Henry heard Fitzwilliam's booming voice.

"Come outside, man," Fitzwilliam said. "I won't step into a hovel such as this."

Henry heard Snidefellow answer that the duchess would not appreciate the insult, as she had built the cottage especially for his convenience.

Despite Snidefellow's protests, Henry heard the front door open and close. The councilman had gone outside.

Henry jiggled the latch on the back window, flinching as the iron made a rasping sound. He paused. Fitzwilliam was loudly discussing the possible fates of a councilman who overstepped his bounds. He recounted the tale of a London councilman who had the temerity to accuse the queen's treasurer of corruption and who now made his home in the Tower.

Henry played with the latch again and it came free. He opened the window wide, hoisted himself up, and climbed inside.

Snidefellow's cottage was sparse. For all the man's airs, he lived simply. A low and smoky fireplace took up one wall, his bedstead was pushed up against another, and a plain wood desk took up a third.

Henry tiptoed to the desk. A report to the district council lay on top. Henry read it and was surprised to find that it made no mention of Sir Richard. For all the council would learn from it, nothing of note had occurred in the hamlet of Barton Commons.

He cautiously opened the drawers. One was filled with a stack of parchments; copies of reports scribbled out in spidery handwriting. From the looks of it, Snidefellow reported every doing in the village to the district council, right down to suspecting Farmer Giles of harboring traitorous tendencies due to his gruff manner and lack of civility to the councilman himself. That made it doubly suspicious that the most current report said nothing about Sir Richard. The other drawer only contained ink and quills.

Out front, Fitzwilliam bellowed, "If even a hair on my friend's head is hurt, I'll put you in front of a London magistrate and then we'll see how you answer for yourself."

Snidefellow's slippery voice said, "Your histrionics will get you nowhere. Unlike Sir Richard, I have nothing to hide."

Hide. Maybe Snidefellow had hidden something. Henry peeked up the chimney. He tested the floorboards, feeling for one that was loose. He got on his hands and knees and peered beneath the bedstead. A metal strongbox lay underneath.

Henry dragged it out. It wasn't heavy, so it was not filled with coin. He examined the clasp. It was padlocked.

The latch on the front door rose.

"We can have nothing further to discuss," Snidefellow said. "You will learn the truth about your friend at trial. Good day, sir."

Henry scooped up the box, ran to the window, and threw himself out. He landed with a thud on the grass and reached up and pulled the window closed as the door creaked open.

Hunched over, Henry ran to the woods and mounted Cantankerous. He hurried through the forest, balancing the box on his saddle. Cantankerous's ears were up and her mouth frothing, as if she had been the one to execute the break-in. Henry made the wide U through the woods. As he came to the final turn, Cantankerous moved ever faster, but Henry felt himself relax. He was almost home.

A flash of dark material caught his eye. The pony halted of his own accord and sidestepped, nearly throwing Henry off. He rebalanced the box in his lap and stared at the spot. Could it be Red Callahan?

A face peered from around a tree. A long and gaunt and familiar face.

Henry froze.

It was his father.

Their eyes met. They stared at each other for a moment, then his father turned and disappeared into the trees.

Why was his father here? Why had he not said anything? Where had the man gone?

Henry spurred Cantankerous toward the manor.

As Henry neared the stables, he took a deep breath and tried to analyze the situation. Of course, his parents wanted him back so they could sell him off. All they ever thought about was money and to them Henry was just a commodity. A farmer sold eggs, his parents sold him. But how had they tracked him to Hampshire? Were they both here, or just his father? Why was his father hiding in the Queen's Forest?

His father had seen him get into the carriage in London, but how could he have discovered anything after that? He and Sir Richard had been in a public coach with no identifying marks when they made their way to the Angel. Even Sir Richard's private carriage did not have a coat of arms or anything that would hint at who it belonged to.

Perhaps the baker, Mr. Clemens, had let it slip that

Henry had been on his way to apply for the position as Sir Richard's assistant? If that had been the case, his father could have easily purchased a newspaper and read the advertisement for himself. Henry remembered clearly enough that it stated: *Barton Commons, Hampshire.*

Those times when Henry had felt like he was being watched and had sensed danger, he had been right. His instincts had tried to tell him there was danger lurking nearby. But why had his father only been watching him? Why the secrecy? His mother and father had a rightful claim to him. The law didn't care whether parents were kind or cruel. So why did his father turn and disappear into the woods when he spotted Henry, instead of grabbing him and hauling him back to London?

Henry resolved that he would do his best to help Sir Richard. Then he would run somewhere that his parents would fear to follow. He would stow away on a ship to America. It had been his plan before he had heard of Sir Richard's advertisement. It would have to be his plan again. His parents would not dare follow him to America.

His heart sank as he thought of Matilda. He would have to leave her behind. The first creature that had ever counted on him and loved him and now he would have to abandon her. He couldn't even explain to her why it must be so, that it wouldn't be fair to drag her from place to place, neither of them assured of food or a bed. He knew what it was like to be anchorless; he did not want Matilda to know, too. He just wished there was a way she could understand his reasons for leaving her.

Henry felt lightheaded. He had thought he'd finally found his place in the world. But soon, he would be floating around anchorless again.

His job right now was to help Sir Richard. Whatever his parents' plans were, they would not swoop in and grab him this minute or they would have done it already. Knowing them, they probably hoped to somehow squeeze some money out of Sir Richard and were biding their time and waiting for an opportunity.

Behind the stable, Henry dismounted and pushed the strongbox under some bushes. He walked Cantankerous around to the doors and handed the reins to Bertram, then ran back to collect the box and hurried into the manor. As he jogged down the main hall toward the laboratory, he met Fitzwilliam coming in the front door with a stranger.

Henry stopped in his tracks.

"Nothing to fear, Henry," Fitzwilliam said. "This is Mr. Candlewick, Sir Richard's solicitor."

The solicitor was a small man with receding black hair and wire-rimmed spectacles. He wore a dark and somber coat and an even more somber expression. "The letter writer, I presume?" he asked in a soft voice.

"Yes, sir," Henry answered.

Mr. Candlewick stared at the box in Henry's hands. Henry said, "This is just something that Mr. Fitzwilliam needed."

"Unfortunately," Mr. Candlewick said, "I have already been apprised of where that box came from."

Henry did not think the solicitor looked very approving, but there was nothing to be done about it. "It's locked," he said to Fitzwilliam.

Fitzwilliam herded them into the laboratory. He grabbed the box from Henry's arms. He laid it on the desk, unsheathed his dagger and started working on the lock. "Good going, Henry," he said. "Though I would have happily changed places with you. Burglary has to be more pleasant than conversing with that conniving creature."

"Mr. Fitzwilliam," Mr. Candlewick said, "I must again protest this unseemly, well frankly this illegal, method of investigation."

Henry had thought that was what the solicitor would say about breaking into Snidefellow's cottage. Still, now that he'd done it he couldn't say he was sorry about it.

"Quite right of you to think it," Fitzwilliam said to the solicitor, "you being a law man and all that. As I am not a law man, I'm not at all troubled by it."

Fitzwilliam broke the lock. Despite Mr. Candlewick's reluctance to be involved in the theft, he came closer to peer inside the strongbox.

The box was tightly packed with layers of parchment. "You've got it, Henry," Fitzwilliam said. "If there is any evidence to be found against that scoundrel, it's bound to be in here."

**143**

Henry was relieved. The box had been so light he had almost feared it was empty.

Fitzwilliam turned to the solicitor. "I suggest you take the carriage to see Sir Richard. While you are interviewing him, Henry and I will sort through these papers. We will acquaint you with anything relevant we discover when you return. There will be no need to acquaint you with how we came by the information, thus absolving you of any involvement with our investigative techniques."

Fitzwilliam removed the parchments and divided them into two piles. Henry sat down and thumbed through his stack. Most were official council correspondence about a change to this rule or that rule. There was a commendation for Mr. Snidefellow's excellent service. The next parchment was brief, but Henry would recognize the handwriting anywhere. He scanned to the bottom.

Bartholomew Hewitt.

His father.

The letter read: *You may very well advise patience, but we are starving in this Godforsaken city. We'll sell the boy to a sweep as you suggested, but that won't take us very far. If we don't hear that you're to marry soon, then caution to the wind—we're coming to claim what's ours.*

Henry's hands shook as he fumbled through the rest,

searching for more correspondence from his father. He found one other, dated just the month before.

*The brat has got away. When I saw him last, he was getting into a carriage. I was able to discover that he had applied as an assistant to a Sir Richard Blackstone, of your very neighborhood. The man lives right next door to you know who. The game is up. We must act now.*

Henry buried the letters in the pile. How did his parents know Snidefellow? *Why* did they know him? What did they want to claim? What game was up? Sir Richard only had one neighbor—the duchess. Why would his father refer to the duchess as "you know who"?

Fitzwilliam threw his last letter down. "Nothing here," he said. "Just a bunch of drivel from the district council and a couple of letters from Snidefellow's father, claiming he doesn't send enough money, which I'm sure is true."

"Nothing interesting here either," Henry said softly.

Mrs. Splunket bustled into the room. "I didn't hear you come in," she said to Henry. "A note was delivered. A note from the duchess herself."

Mrs. Splunket proudly held out the folded paper. Henry took it and broke the seal. Fitzwilliam looked over Henry's shoulder as he read it.

*Henry—I have sent multiple requests to Mr. Snidefellow directing him to attend me. He has not come here, nor has he answered my messages. Something is very wrong.*

Henry laid down the letter. The duchess was right,

something was very wrong. If Snidefellow would not even respond to an invitation from the duchess, there was something else going on. Something he did not understand.

Henry and Fitzwilliam spent the next hours speculating on why Snidefellow would ignore a summons from the duchess. Henry privately wondered if it had something to do with his father's arrival. Their musings were briefly interrupted by lunch, which was a joint of mutton carelessly thrown on a plate. Mrs. Splunket explained that she was too distraught to accomplish anything more.

The solicitor returned in the late afternoon. The man was pale and haggard. He sank into a chair and said, "The trial begins tomorrow."

# CHAPTER ELEVEN

"The trial starts tomorrow!" Henry said.

"Can they do that?" Fitzwilliam asked. "You've had no time to prepare a case."

"A magistrate may order an expeditious trial, if it is deemed necessary," Mr. Candlewick said, "but this is most unusual as I see no cause for inordinate speed. I attempted to reason with the fellow, to remind him of professional courtesy and all that, but he wouldn't hear of it. I pointed out that technically, I could not try the case, as I'm a solicitor, not a barrister. He waved off that requirement too. Most extraordinary."

"Will they transfer Sir Richard to Winchester?" Henry asked.

"No," Candlewick answered. "The case will be heard here. For matters that in any way involve the church, it is permitted to hold the trial locally. The magistrate says that as the accusations against Sir Richard include a claim that he does the devil's work, that does involve the church and so he exercises his right to keep it here, rather than transfer. A circuit prosecutor will arrive this evening. I am wondering what the circuit prosecutor will make of all this; it is very strange, indeed."

They spent the night in the dining room. Mr. Candlewick scribbled notes while Henry, Mrs. Splunket, and Fitzwilliam told him everything they knew. Except for how the whole mess had begun. When the solicitor asked if there had been any unusual happenings around the manor, Henry caught Mrs. Splunket's eye and shook his head no. He did not think a London lawyer would cope very well with a story about a giant tarantula and powder from a magical Amazonian tree.

After all had been said, they sat in silence while Fitzwilliam and the solicitor sipped their port.

Henry got up to go find Matilda. He thought it strange that she had not been at his feet during dinner as she generally liked to wait there, hoping for something to drop.

He entered the kitchen to see if she were sleeping on her bed. Bertram sat on the floor with a pile of shredded beef next to him. He held up a piece and Matilda stood wagging her tail. Bertram held it just above her nose and said, "Sit."

As Matilda's eyes gazed higher at the looming meat, her back end naturally went down.

"There you go, girl," Bertram said. "You've done it." He noticed Henry and said, "I'm just teachin' her some tricks. She's a clever dog."

Henry thought the same himself. Matilda had recently

figured out how to open Henry's bedchamber door by getting up on her hind legs and knocking at the knob with her paw. He sat down and said, "She is clever, I think. Now that she's gained weight, it's like she's gotten smarter."

"That's what care and attention will do for an animal," Bertram said. "I knew the moment I set eyes on her that she was primed for a miraculous recovery."

"Bertram," Henry said, "if I ever had to go away, you would see to it that Matilda would be all right, wouldn't you?"

"I'd guard this dog with my life, I would. Why? You plannin' on going somewhere?"

"Oh, no," Henry said. "I just thought as a responsible dog owner I should make arrangements. You never know what could happen."

"I suppose you never do know," Bertram said. "It'd be a shame though, as I was just gettin' used to you being around. I might have even gone around tellin' people that my idea that you were the son of a common pirate turned out to be mistaken."

"And also that I was raised in the depraved alleys of London," Henry added.

"Aye, that too."

"Thank you, Bertram," Henry said. "I really appreciate that you cleared those stories up."

"Don't be thanking me now," Bertram said gruffly. "Everybody knows you can't be a responsible dog owner and a pirate. Just common sense, is what it is."

Bertram hauled himself to his feet and reluctantly said good night to Matilda. He even said good night to Henry. Matilda followed Henry back to the dining room.

The puppy retrieved a beef bone she had hidden away in the corner of the room and sat herself down at Henry's feet. She ferociously shook the bone, dropped it and stared at it, covered it with her paw and then took it up again, her tail thumping on the carpet. Silence hung over the room like a pall, and Matilda was the only resident of the household who appeared to be enjoying the evening. Henry would be heartbroken to have to leave her behind; she was the best friend he'd ever had. No matter what he did or said, Matilda always heartily approved. He consoled himself with the knowledge that she would be well cared for at the manor. Bertram and Mrs. Splunket would see to that. Between the coachman and the housekeeper, his dog would be the most pampered in all of England.

Matilda had been small and nervous when Henry had first adopted her, but with care she had grown. From the looks of her fat, round belly, she would grow more still. All she had needed was kindness to make her transformation. Bertram was right, she had made a miraculous recovery.

Henry sat up suddenly with a startling idea: Fitzwilliam had made a miraculous recovery, too. Mr. Terrible got crickets. It was so obvious. He knew how the lupuna powder worked.

"Well," Mr. Candlewick said, stretching his legs and rising to his feet, "it's almost midnight. The proceedings begin

**150**

at nine sharp. The only helpful thing we can do now is get a decent night's sleep."

Henry was hustled to his room by Mrs. Splunket as she said softly, "I never knowed a boy to be up so late. We'll be lucky if you don't catch a fever from it."

He tried to tell her about the lupuna powder, but she shushed him and said he sounded delirious already.

Henry was bursting to tell Fitzwilliam about his theory, but the trial was just hours away. It would have to wait.

He lay awake for an hour, rolling his theory around and looking at it from all sides. His idea wasn't foolproof, he decided. But at least it had some logic to it. He felt sure he must be right.

The next morning, they climbed the steps of the church. The solicitor said, "The only defense I can muster in so short a time is to keep hammering at the utter lunacy of the accusations and paint Snidefellow as a disappointed and vengeful suitor."

Henry, Fitzwilliam, and Mr. Candlewick made their way to the front of the church. As Henry had expected, it was packed with onlookers. Whole families crowded the pews and the overflow stood at the back of the church. The trial would be a public spectacle. It was the biggest event in Barton Commons since the kidnapping of the duchess's son.

Sir Richard weakly smiled at their approach. The duchess sat on the other side of Sir Richard, having placed herself in a position that would resolve any questions about where her loyalty lay.

The magistrate was up on the altar, flanked by his constables. Mr. Snidefellow sat in the front pew on the opposite side of the church. The duchess glared at him until his cheeks colored.

The magistrate banged his gavel and said, "Bailiff, read the charges."

The old bailiff held a parchment in front of him. "Sir Richard Blackstone is hereby charged with the practice of witchcraft, which has unleashed a padfoot and caused the death of Red Callahan. Further, he is charged with the kidnapping of William St. John, son of the Duke and Duchess of St. John."

Henry glanced around the church to see what effect the charges had. Most of the audience had an eager look, as if they were about to see a play. Mr. Small, the curate, looked horrified.

The magistrate said, "Mr. Egbert Joswell will argue the charges for the Crown."

Henry peered over at the wigged prosecutor. Mr. Joswell's red face sat atop a short and round body; he reminded Henry of a fall apple.

Mr. Candlewick rose and said, "May I have the courtesy of having a word with Mr. Joswell before we begin?"

"No," the magistrate said. "Mr. Joswell, you may proceed."

Henry watched Snidefellow hand the prosecutor a sheaf of parchments.

Mr. Joswell shuffled up to the dais. "Your Honor," he said in a gravelly voice, peering down at the papers, "This case is about putting the pieces together. All the pieces taken together will show that Sir Richard Blackstone did knowingly make mischief in the village of Barton Commons.

"First," the prosecutor said, "Sir Richard arrives unexpectedly in the neighborhood. Unlike other gentlemen, he is never seen in church. He keeps to himself and rarely receives callers."

Henry leaned forward and whispered into Candlewick's ear, "He always receives the duchess, but tries never to receive Snidefellow."

Candlewick nodded.

"He transformed a perfectly innocent drawing room into a secretive laboratory," the prosecutor continued. "He refuses social invitations, including the duchess's own dusk-to-dawn croquet party which everyone knows is the crowning event of the season. Further, on the night of the croquet party, an unearthly creature is seen by a footman. Sir Richard and his London urchin were observed riding around in the dark, waving torches at it. And then, a good man goes missing."

Henry whispered, "Sir Richard hates croquet and Red Callahan is a drunkard."

"Red Callahan has been pronounced dead by Your

Honor," Mr. Joswell continued, "on account of everybody knows he could not stay away from The Buck and Boar for days at a time. His liver would not hold up."

Mr. Candlewick jumped to his feet. "Objection, Your Honor. A man cannot be pronounced dead merely because he has not been seen at a pub."

"I've had it from a respected physician that I certainly can come to that conclusion. Objection overruled," the magistrate said.

Henry twisted his hands together. It wasn't only the prosecutor who was taking direction from Snidefellow; the magistrate was too.

"The man is dead," the prosecutor said, "just days after a padfoot is seen. Blackstone claims to search for Callahan and, instead, he conveniently returns with a footprint from the duchess's own missing son."

Henry wanted to whisper some kind of information to Candlewick, but he didn't know what to say. He couldn't very well tell the solicitor that they found the footprint while they searched the cave to find out if Red Callahan had been liquefied by the tarantula.

"How does Sir Richard find a footprint in the cave, when that cave has already been gone over with a fine-toothed comb? The answer is, he didn't. He sought the duchess's hand in marriage to protect him from the accusations against him and, to seal the deal, he presents her with the footprint he had in his possession all along."

Mr. Joswell turned with a flourish to the villagers. "The kidnappers would have wanted ample evidence that they had the boy. That footprint remained in Blackstone's possession all these years because he, Sir Richard Blackstone, is the kidnapper!"

The audience gasped. Henry didn't think the story held up very well, but the villagers seemed to follow Mr. Joswell's logic completely.

The duchess's face had gone from pink to white. Sir Richard sat stone-faced.

"So you see," Mr. Joswell said, "each piece taken together brings us to the truth, that Blackstone is the devil's agent. This calls for one punishment: death by hanging. The prosecution rests."

The magistrate said, "Mr. Candlewick. Proceed with your defense."

Henry bit his lip. The solicitor would have to make a strong case on Sir Richard's behalf.

Mr. Candlewick rose. "Your Honor, as Mr. Joswell has so helpfully pointed out, each piece of evidence on its own signifies nothing. Let us go through them one by one. Sir Richard unexpectedly arrives. Yes, he was given a knighthood by our queen and gifted the manor. Where else *would* he arrive? Sir Richard does not attend church. Perhaps, but it does not mean that Sir Richard is not a Godly man. Sir Richard does not receive callers. As you can see," he said, pointing to Fitzwilliam, "he at this very moment has a houseguest. He has received the duchess on numerous occasions. He makes every effort *not* to receive Mr. Snidefellow because he doesn't like the man. I suspect Sir Richard is not alone in his dislike of the councilman, who has shown himself to be an oily, arrogant, and nosy individual."

The room erupted in laughter.

"As to Sir Richard having transformed a sitting room into a laboratory," Mr. Candlewick continued, "what gentleman does not engage in scientific pursuits?"

Henry heard a man behind him mutter, "That's true enough. These gentry types got to fill up the days somehow."

"And," Mr. Candlewick said, "to imply that Sir Richard had some dark purpose for not attending the dusk-to-dawn croquet party is absurd. Sir Richard does not like to play croquet."

Henry began to feel more optimistic. Mr. Candlewick was picking apart the Crown's case.

"And what of this supposed creature?" Mr. Candlewick asked. "Only one person claims to have seen the alleged beast. A footman who believes he has gone mad. It is my experience that when a person tells you they have gone mad, you would do well to believe it.

"And why was Sir Richard riding around in the dark? I will point out that it was *just barely* dark, not midnight. May a gentleman not appear on horseback after sunset these days without running the risk of being arrested?

"And how did Sir Richard find the boy's footprint? He

was in the cave searching for Red Callahan. Ground shifts over time, so a thing hidden may suddenly come to light. What woman has not lost a thimble and conducted a thorough search, only to conclude that it is well and truly gone? And yet, when it mysteriously appears again . . . is that the devil's work, or is that just the nature of lost items?

"And that brings us to the matter of Red Callahan himself. He is a well-known drunkard and there is not a shred of evidence that he is dead. For all we know, he's sitting in a tavern in Winchester as we speak.

"Further, the idea that Sir Richard Blackstone, wholly unknown in these parts until three years ago, is somehow connected to the kidnapping of William St. John is a ludicrous notion. At the time of the kidnapping, Sir Richard was attending Oxford and had never set foot in this county.

"Finally, I will contend that Mr. Snidefellow, the author of all this poppycock, is merely a rejected lover intent upon vengeance. He sought to woo the duchess and was quite rightly dismissed. He is driven to a fury by Sir Richard's success in the matter. He has abused his authority as councilman in the most abominable fashion. If there is any evil here, look to Snidefellow for it."

The duchess sat straight, her lips pressed into a straight line. Henry did not think she liked her private life talked about so publicly. Snidefellow had gone red up to his ears.

The crowd behind Henry was agitated. He leaned back to hear what they were saying.

**157**

"Snidefellow and the duchess! That ladder-climbin' rascal. As if her Ladyship would connect herself to a councilman! I bet he did make the whole thing up outta spite."

Mr. Candlewick had managed to turn people's minds in Sir Richard's favor. The magistrate glanced at Snidefellow and shrugged his shoulders, as if to say, "What can I do about it?"

All at once, the back of the church was in an uproar. "It's him! It's Red! He ain't dead!"

The magistrate slumped in his chair. Mr. Snidefellow clenched his fists.

Henry stood up to get a better view. Red Callahan stumbled into the church, thin and haggard.

Mr. Candlewick said, "Is this the man who was supposedly murdered? Bring him forward, I demand to question him."

Red Callahan was hauled to the front of the church and sworn in.

"Please tell this court," Mr. Candlewick said, "where you have been hiding yourself."

Red Callahan broke down. In between sobs, he said, "I was walkin' home from The Buck and Boar, the same walk I done these past twenty years. All of a sudden I see a monstrous spider standin' on the road. Black and hairy and as big as a house. It had all these eyes starin' at me and it comes toward me and I ran. The thing chased me through the woods and all the while I was runnin' I was thinkin', Red, this has to be the drink. This has to be the tremens giving

**158**

you these visions. But even though I told myself it weren't real, it seemed so real that I couldn't stop myself. I ran and ran 'til I couldn't run no more. I was lost in the woods and I lay next to a stream all them nights, fearin' a creature of my own mind. The tremens left me this mornin' and I found my way out. I swear on the Lord's name, I'll never drink another drop of liquor."

Mary had gone in pursuit of Red after all. The poor fellow, he must have been scared out of his wits. Henry smiled. Snidefellow's case had just fallen apart.

Snidefellow jumped to his feet. "Blackstone may not have killed Red Callahan, but we have just heard of another creature!"

A man behind Henry snorted and said, "Now we're to believe in giant spiders? What next? Mice the size of dogs?"

The magistrate banged his gavel. With a heavy sigh, he said, "Having discovered that Red Callahan is not dead, and so was not killed by a padfoot, and having no evidence of what Red really saw that caused him to flee, and having no evidence other than a footprint as to the kidnapping, this court deems that the charges are dis—"

A loud buzzing sound filled the church.

# CHAPTER TWELVE

**H**enry gripped the pew and hoped that buzzing sound wasn't what he thought it was.

The ponderous housefly flew through the open church doors.

The villagers turned toward the sound. Men shouted and girls screamed. Red Callahan turned pale and cried, "Not another one!" An elderly woman near the front of the church said, "For the love of heaven," and dropped into a faint.

The fly landed on the pulpit and mechanically washed its face with its long front legs. It rubbed over the two protrusions on the front of its mouth, and then a long tongue rolled out and felt around the top of the pulpit.

The curate crossed himself and backed away from it. Two heavyset farmers left the church and came back wielding shovels. They charged up to the altar, each man taking a side. When they were within striking distance, both men raised their shovels. As their arms swung down to crush the beast, it took to the air. The shovels rang down on the pulpit.

The fly buzzed over the villagers' heads, knocking into walls. The farmers chased it, swinging their shovels and putting holes in the plaster. They cornered it, and with a large splat, it fell to the ground. One of the farmers scooped it up and carried it to the front of the church.

That stupid fly! Henry felt a wave of regret wash over him. He should have done something about the fly. He should have lured it in with honey and trapped it. He should have tried something, other than just hope it had been eaten by a falcon.

The magistrate banged his gavel and shouted, "Order!"

Snidefellow leapt up on the altar. "There! You have your proof! There can be no denying that Sir Richard Blackstone is guilty. A creature from hell has been sent through these very church doors to confirm it."

The magistrate turned to Mr. Candlewick. "Do you have anything you would say to this?"

Mr. Candlewick looked grave. He rose and said, "Your Honor, I do not know the meaning of that insect. I would ask the court to consider a scientific explanation. Perhaps it is a new species, or it has been affected by some type of corrupted water or food. In any event, there is no more evidence that it is connected to Sir Richard than it is connected to anyone in this church."

"If you've nothing further," the magistrate said, "I will hear closing arguments on the morrow." He turned to his constables and said, "Admit that monstrosity to evidence."

**161**

A constable approached Sir Richard to take him back to the jail. Before he allowed himself to be led away, Sir Richard whispered something to the duchess. She glanced in Henry's direction and nodded her head.

Fitzwilliam leaned over and said, "To the manor. Quickly. We have a mere twenty-four hours to devise a plan."

In the library, Fitzwilliam and Mr. Candlewick debated the best course of action. Fitzwilliam was all for a prison break and taking Sir Richard abroad. They would flee to Rome until the whole mess could be unraveled. Mr. Candlewick felt that would be ill-advised. He counseled that running to the Continent would present a look of guilt. He proposed that if the decision went against them, he would ride to Winchester and appeal.

The duchess swept into the room. Henry had not heard the door and suspected she had not bothered to knock.

The men leapt to their feet, but the duchess waved them down. "Before Sir Richard was led away," she said, looking directly at Henry, "he directed me to see you. He gave me the following message: 'Henry, you are to tell the duchess everything. From start to finish. Everything, with no exceptions.'"

"Everything?" Henry stammered. "Are you sure he meant actually everything?"

"Quite sure," she said.

"But," Henry said, glancing at Fitzwilliam, "everything is a lot. Not even Mr. Candlewick knows everything."

Mr. Candlewick sighed. "Good grief. There's more?"

"I'm afraid so, sir," Henry said.

"Well, if any of it will go against Sir Richard, I don't want to hear it," the solicitor said. "Henry, perhaps you should step outside with Her Grace while Fitzwilliam and I continue our conference."

Henry led the duchess to the back garden. She attempted to sit on the low wall encircling the fountain, but Henry shouted, "No! Don't sit there!"

The duchess sprang up and said, "Why ever not?"

"There are piranhas in there," he said. "They've got sharp teeth and they'll go for a finger if you get too close."

The duchess turned to stare at the murky water. "Why does Sir Richard have such a thing in his fountain?"

"Fitzwilliam brought them back from the Amazon and this was the only place to put them," Henry said. "I'm not sure what he will do with them in winter, though he's talked about building a giant aquarium for the dining room."

"Indeed," the duchess said. She did not look too enthusiastic about the idea.

Henry showed the duchess into the gazebo. She sat on a bench and arranged her gown around her, then stared at Henry in silence.

"You're certain Sir Richard said I was to tell you all?" Henry asked. "Completely all?"

"All," she said in a determined tone.

Henry told the duchess everything that had happened, watching her expression closely. She was amused by the idea that Sir Richard had tried to turn a tarantula yellow for her cousin's birthday. Why he thought the queen would like a tarantula of any color, she couldn't guess. She was even more amused that the tarantula was called Mary, Queen of Scots. She was less amused when she heard how Sir Richard's experiment on the tarantula had turned out. Henry hurried on, hoping that if he said everything extremely fast, it wouldn't sound as bad as it actually was. He ended by assuring her that Mary was safely trapped in the valley beyond the cave, hoping that would end the tale on a high note.

"And that's it?" she asked.

"That's it." Henry had not told her about spotting his father or discovering that his parents had some sort of a connection to Snidefellow. He figured she would not be interested in the problems of a commoner.

"Red Callahan was not having visions from delirium tremens after all. He really did see what he was afraid he'd seen. I don't know what we're to do," she said, twisting a silver bracelet on her wrist. "I had thought I would go to London and petition my cousin, but if the queen discovers there is an unnatural creature wandering around the place, things will go very badly for Sir Richard. She is as superstitious as a gypsy. My second idea was to dismiss Snidefellow, but I would have to give the district council a reason. Now that there is an oversized fly admitted to evidence I don't dare do it. Our only chance is to make the evidence vanish. But even if we could somehow steal the fly carcass, that tarantula will be found. There has been too much talk about the kidnapping and, in consequence, the cave. Sooner or later someone will go there, find the blockade and open it up."

Henry was rather surprised that the duchess would consider stealing. She was right, though. Making the evidence vanish was their only hope.

"What are you thinking of?" the duchess asked. "Out with it."

"I'm pretty sure I've figured out how the lupuna powder works," Henry said. "If I'm right, I can return both creatures to their original size."

"Then we've no time to lose. I'm off this instant to change into my riding clothes. I shall meet you out front on horseback. Then, we go to the cave."

"Wait," Henry said. "You want to go to the cave?"

"Who else should go but Sir Richard's fiancée?"

"What about Fitzwilliam and Mr. Candlewick?" Henry asked. "Maybe they should go."

"Bah," the duchess said, rising from the bench. "Let those men continue their conference. What we need now is action."

Henry stared at her.

The duchess smiled. "Did you know that the duke and I

once slipped into Paris on a spying mission for the Crown? It was highly dangerous." She paused, as if lost in memory. Then she said, "We were nearly caught. I quite enjoyed myself."

The duchess strode away, her silk gown billowing out behind her.

Henry sat for a few moments. He had thought that once he told the duchess everything, she would faint and he would have to revive her with smelling salts. She was related to royalty, which made her practically a princess. From the stories he'd read in Sir Richard's library, he had been under the impression that while a princess was always kind, she would generally swoon in the face of danger. While she was fainting, the knight would spring into action and save the day. He supposed the stories had got it wrong.

Henry had the lupuna powder and a glove tucked safely in his pocket. He had passed the library on his way to the laboratory to get it, but did not stop to tell the solicitor or Fitzwilliam where he was going. The men were still hotly debating what to do if the verdict went against Sir Richard on the morrow.

The duchess met him on the drive, astride an eighteen-hand chestnut. He supposed that if she had the nerve to get on such a beast, she must be a skilled horsewoman.

Henry had borrowed Real Beauty. He wouldn't have

time to drag Cantankerous out of his stall or spend half the day urging him to move faster. Cantankerous had eyed him darkly when he passed by the stall, and whinnied when he left. If the pony really liked going places, he had a strange way of showing it.

"To the cave," the duchess said. She wheeled her horse around and spurred him into a canter.

They rode in silence until they passed the post road. Henry took the horses into the trees and tied them off.

Henry led the way up the slope to the clearing in front of the cave. At the entrance, he lit a torch and peered in. The rock wall that he and Sir Richard had built still held.

Stepping through the silk burrow that Mary had left behind, Henry showed the duchess where her son's footprint had been found. She knelt down and ran her fingers over the dirt, but she did not let herself indulge in any weepiness. She stood up and said, "Tell me about this lupuna tree."

"The natives that Fitzwilliam traveled with through the Amazon jungle believe the lupuna tree is powerful," Henry said. "They told Fitzwilliam that if the tree was offended, the person who delivered the insult would be punished. When Fitzwilliam was ill, he leaned against a lupuna tree and the natives were frightened for him. But then, Fitzwilliam was cured instead of harmed. So I thought to myself, why would the tree cure Fitzwilliam instead of turning him into a giant? And then when I accidentally got some powder on Mr. Terrible—"

"Who?"

"The Phyllobates terribilis," Henry said. "The poisonous frog in Sir Richard's laboratory."

"Good grief."

"Yes, well, Mr. Terrible did not turn into a giant either. He got an aquarium full of crickets, which he happily ate. So Fitzwilliam and the frog went well, and then the tarantula and the fly went . . . not as well."

The duchess nodded her head. "And so, why the different results?"

"The only thing I can figure is it has to be intent. Fitzwilliam said he read part of a poem: 'Mother Earth and Brother Tree, I love thee well, watch over me.' See? Fitzwilliam paid tribute to the tree. Mr. Terrible was just an innocent bystander; he wasn't trying to make the tree do anything and I wasn't either, as I just accidentally spilled the powder. But Sir Richard was using the tree for his own purposes."

"So the lupuna tree decided it would teach Sir Richard a lesson?"

"That's what I think," Henry said. "And the lesson happened to be the massive growth of the tarantula because it's the *giant* lupuna tree. Same thing with the fly."

"Well, who are we to know what goes on in these foreign places?" the duchess mused. "I have heard there are men in India who can levitate right off the ground. You won't find an Englishman aimlessly floating around. But now that we have a theory, what will we do about it?"

"I was thinking about throwing some powder on Mary and reciting the poem," Henry said. "Maybe that would undo everything."

The duchess was pensive. "While I follow your logic, it seems a somewhat dicey plan to throw powder on a giant spider and then read it a poem."

"I know," Henry said. "But it's my only idea."

"You would have to get dangerously close to it. You may not succeed."

"I have to try," Henry said. "Sir Richard rescued me off the streets, and he's been very kind, and he gave me my own room that is actually in the house and let me have the smallest puppy and well, he's the first person to ever . . ." Henry trailed off, not really knowing how to explain all that Sir Richard had done for him.

"Say no more, Henry," she said. "I understand it all; you're a steadfast young man. Now, I did not come to sit idly by. I will distract the creature so that you may approach unnoticed."

Henry argued against this idea as well as he could. He could not imagine what would happen if the duchess were injured. Or worse, liquefied. But she was decided.

The duchess helped him dismantle the wall until she was covered in dirt from head to toe. Henry began to feel more comfortable around her now that they were working together and she no longer looked so much like a duchess.

They removed enough of the stone to create an opening they could squeeze through.

Henry climbed out and the duchess followed behind.

The valley was empty. Henry scanned the area where he had last seen Mary. The grass was still packed down from where she had sat, but there was no sign of her. He examined the steep valley walls. Every wall but the one leading to the cave was impossible to climb. Had she reverted to her original size? Henry had not thought of that possibility, but the effects of the lupuna powder certainly could be temporary.

"You're certain there actually was a giant tarantula?" the duchess said. "It wasn't something you imagined? It would be entirely understandable in a boy your age. You might have seen that white substance in the cave and attributed it to the silk of a giant spider, when it could be from something else entirely."

"Not my imagination. She was here," Henry said. "Look, you can still see the outline where she sat."

The duchess squinted her eyes at the opposite end of the valley. "Then that means she could be anywhere. I don't know how your Mary, Queen of Scots, has escaped, but she is well and truly gone."

As Henry scanned the sides of the valley and thought about where they might search for the tarantula, pressure slammed into his temples and he was lifted off his feet.

# CHAPTER THIRTEEN

**H**enry clutched at the fangs on either side of his head. The spider loomed over him. She had been lying in wait, crouched above the entrance.

"Hold on, Henry," the duchess cried, grasping at his swinging legs.

Henry let go of a fang and reached into his pocket. The pressure was immense; he felt his skull could shatter at any moment. He yanked out the packet of powder.

The duchess grabbed it from his hands and crawled up the slope toward the tarantula.

"The glove," Henry cried and threw it to her.

She caught the glove and wrestled it on. The duchess reached into the sack, clutched a handful of powder and threw it on the spider. "Recite the poem!" she cried.

Henry shouted, "Mother Earth and Brother Tree, I love thee well, watch over me!"

Mary released her grip and Henry fell to the ground.

The duchess helped him to his feet. He felt a soft plop on the top of his head.

The duchess pulled the spider from his hair. She held it in the palm of her gloved hand. "Listen here, Queen of the Scots, that is quite enough mayhem from you, madam."

Henry peered at the spider. Mary sat docile in the duchess's hand, her eight eyes looking somewhat perplexed.

He retrieved his satchel from the cave and brought out the box Sir Richard had used to transport her from London. The duchess slipped the tarantula in and Henry secured the lid. "Good work," she said.

Henry flushed. He had done it. His plan had actually worked. Nobody could discover a giant spider and blame it on Sir Richard.

"Now," the duchess said, "we just have to do the same to that blasted fly."

The duchess examined Henry's temples. "The skin is not broken, but bruises are coming up already," she said. "You'll need a likely story about how you got them."

Henry thought for a moment. "I could say I was kicked in the head by my horse," he said.

"Twice?" the duchess asked. "On either side?"

"Twice. His name is Cantankerous. Everybody who knows him will believe it."

The duchess and Henry rode back to the manor at a leisurely pace. The duchess told Henry she had not had as much fun in a long time. She said being a duchess was mostly boring and she would have packed up and gone to America to pioneer the West years ago, if it weren't for holding the dukedom for her son.

At the mention of America, Henry flinched. During the excitement of testing out his theory on Mary, he had been able to forget what was ahead of him. Once Sir Richard was free, Henry would have to run. He would have to make his way to a port and slip onto a ship bound for America. He would stow away as long as he could, but would no doubt be found out before the seven weeks' journey was through. Then he would be indentured to pay off the passage and he was not at all sure how long that would take. But after that, he would be free. All of that was assuming the ship didn't sink in a storm or get taken by pirates. The journey was a terrifying prospect, but it was the only way he knew to be rid of his parents forever.

They reached Sir Richard's drive and the duchess said, "I'll step inside and see how far those men have come in their conference. Whatever they have been jabbering about, it's time for a real plan."

Henry and the duchess entered the library. Fitzwilliam was alone and told them that Mr. Candlewick had taken himself upstairs to compose his closing argument. They had still not agreed on what course of action to take after the trial.

"The problem with you and that solicitor," the duchess said to Fitzwilliam, "is that you are pessimists. You are entirely too focused on what to do when Sir Richard is found guilty. Henry and I have been focused on what to do *before* he is found guilty."

Henry pulled the box from his satchel and showed Fitzwilliam the tarantula.

"By my life, that's good news," Fitzwilliam said, peering into the box. "How did you do it?"

"Henry was very clever in working it all out," the duchess said. "He deduced that the lupuna tree cured you because you honored it with a poem, and it might just cure the spider by doing the same."

"Clever, indeed!" Fitzwilliam paused. "You're certain she's permanently small? She won't suddenly decide to grow again in the middle of the night?"

Henry had not thought of that. "Uh, I hope not."

"No time to worry about that now," the duchess said. "On the morrow, you're to convince Mr. Candlewick to demand to see the evidence, meaning of course, the fly. Once it's produced, you and Henry will walk up with him to examine the thing. Circle round it, blocking the onlookers' view. Throw the powder on it and recite the poem."

"Your Grace," Henry said, "the one problem I see is that the villagers have already viewed the fly in its bigger state. How will we explain the change?"

"The facts in front of them will be what they rely on,"

**174**

Fitzwilliam said. "Candlewick's proposal that there must be a scientific reason will seem the most likely thing. It can be done, I should think. On my sail to South America, some of the crew took a terrible fright in the predawn hours of the morning. They claimed to have seen a kraken. Whether they did or did not, I never knew. But what I did know was a frightened crew is a dangerous crew. Later that day, I spotted a mass of seaweed floating atop the sea and said, 'Gentlemen, there's your kraken.' They were only too happy to believe it."

The church was packed in anticipation of Sir Richard's verdict. Henry's stomach had been twisting in knots all morning. He would have one chance to transform the fly. He had to get it right.

The duchess caught his eye and winked at him. She wore her best jewels and sparkled with emeralds and diamonds in the dim church. She laid her hand on Sir Richard's arm and they put their heads together. Henry guessed she was telling him of yesterday's adventure as he watched Sir Richard's face turn from alarm to happiness.

The magistrate entered the courtroom and called for order. He directed Mr. Joswell to proceed with his closing argument.

Joswell, as he had done the day before, read from a parchment that Henry was sure had been written by Snidefellow.

Henry turned to see what effect Joswell's fear-mongering had on the villagers. They were silent and grave. Some pulled their children close, as if a padfoot might even now be at the church doors. Henry strained his neck to see to the very back.

His breath caught. His father's tall frame loomed over the men standing in front of the doors. His mother sat in the last pew, staring at him. She wore an expression Henry was familiar with. She was furious.

Henry turned to face the front of the church as Joswell droned on. It was over for him now. If his parents had hoped to pry some money out of Sir Richard's hands, they must have decided that was hopeless. They would seize him before he could leave the church. He would not even have a chance to stow away to America.

His future rolled out before him. He would be sent to work for the chimney sweep. Or if that fell through, he would be sent down into the mines. Wherever he was forced to go, he could count on long hours, little food, ill treatment, and an early death.

Joswell was ending his speech. Henry had no time to think about his own predicament now. If the only good thing he ever did was help save Sir Richard, at least he would have that memory to carry with him.

"In conclusion," Joswell said, "we ask that Your Honor confer protection on the good people of Barton Commons by rendering a verdict of guilty."

Mr. Candlewick stood up. He glanced at Fitzwilliam, who nodded his head. "Your Honor," Mr. Candlewick said, "before I begin my closing argument, I would ask to view the evidence once more."

The magistrate leaned forward. "You want to see the fly?"

"I do, sir."

The magistrate shrugged and sent a constable to fetch the carcass.

Mr. Candlewick, Fitzwilliam, and Henry moved to block the view of it as it came into the courtroom. As Henry watched the constable carry it in, he realized they needn't have worried. As much as the audience leaned forward to get a look, they wouldn't be able to see over the high rim of the box.

Henry had tucked a small sack of the powder and a glove into the pocket of his breeches. He would casually slip the glove on and reach into the sack without attracting attention.

They leaned over the top of the box and stared at the dead creature. "What now?" Candlewick whispered.

"It's merely a fly," Fitzwilliam said loudly. "What kind of court admits a fly as evidence?"

Henry reached in his pocket and wiggled his fingers into the glove. He opened the sack and brought out a handful of the lupuna powder, sprinkling it over the carcass while he murmured the poem. The carcass shook and shivered, then shrunk in on itself.

"What the devil," Candlewick said.

Fitzwilliam leaned toward the solicitor and whispered, "Keep your wits, man."

Candlewick paused for a moment, then held up the box and tilted it for all to see. "Your Honor, Mr. Fitzwilliam is correct. There is nothing unusual here."

Snidefellow leapt to his feet and ran to the box. He stared down at the now normal-sized housefly. "It's a trick! I saw them do it! They're all in league together. That boy threw something on the creature."

Henry's hands trembled.

"Search his pockets," Snidefellow demanded.

A constable grabbed hold of Henry and dragged him to the altar.

Henry glanced at Sir Richard. The knight's brows were knit, as if he were trying to work out what had happened. The duchess had not told Sir Richard of the plan to shrink the fly. She laid her head on his shoulder.

The constable stared at Henry's gloved hand, then ordered him to turn out his pockets. Henry slowly reached in, and powder sprinkled to the floor.

The church erupted in shouts. "He did throw something on the creature. It must be witchcraft!"

Snidefellow smiled.

The magistrate banged his gavel. "I believe this court has seen enough."

Henry had failed. Sir Richard would be found guilty and Henry would end up right back with his parents, for sale to the first comer. He should never have tried to stay in England. He should have boarded the first boat to America that he could find.

Henry paused. Did Sir Richard really need to be found guilty? Might he not take Sir Richard's place on the scaffold? It would be kinder to all—Sir Richard could marry the duchess, and Henry would escape his miserable future.

He flinched as he imagined the rope being put over his head, and then the fall and the snap of his neck.

But it would be quick. He probably wouldn't even feel it. Or if he did, it would only be for a moment. Then, Sir Richard would be safe forever. Henry had one chance to make that happen.

"Sir!" Henry shouted to the magistrate over the din in the church. "It is true that I threw powder on that creature and returned it to its original size. It is I, not Sir Richard, who must be accused of witchcraft."

"Nonsense," Snidefellow said. "They are a pair."

"No," Henry said. "It was not until I arrived that evil befell Barton Commons. Sir Richard did not know who he dealt with."

Sir Richard shook his head no. Henry ignored him.

"We need not take the word of a boy," Snidefellow said. "He has no proof to back up his claims."

"But I do," Henry said. "I do have proof. I have the very mark of the devil upon me. You will find no such mark on Sir Richard."

Henry leaned down. It seemed incomprehensible that he was about to show the world his toes, when he had spent his entire life hiding them. He pulled off a boot.

His father pushed men out of the way and charged down the aisle. A constable restrained him as he neared the front of the church. "The boy talks nonsense!" he cried. "I am Bartholomew Hewitt, his father. Turn him over to me this instant. He does not know what he says—he's queer in the head."

The duchess and Sir Richard turned to look at the man. Sir Richard looked confused, which did not surprise Henry since he had claimed to be an orphan.

"It's true," Henry said. "That man is my father and well aware of the mark I carry."

Henry yanked off one of his stockings and wiggled his six toes.

All in the front pews stared down at his feet. "He's got six," a woman said.

"By my life," a man cried. "It's true! He's got six toes!"

From the back of the church, Henry's mother shouted, "Run!"

At first Henry didn't understand who his mother was shouting to. Did she want *him* to run? Then he saw Snidefellow dash toward the back of the church, leaping over pews and ducking outstretched hands. The councilman burst out of the doors and disappeared.

Henry's father attempted to follow him, but a constable held him back. Henry's mother fought off a pair of farmers who held her securely.

Henry had always been undecided about how evil his toes really made him. He had hoped that maybe it was just an old wives' tale. But considering that Snidefellow was so terrified that he ran away, Henry had to admit it was true. It really was the mark of the devil.

Sir Richard stood up and pointed to Bartholomew Hewitt. "You are not that boy's father."

Henry's father struggled with the constable who held him.

Sir Richard addressed the onlookers. "It is impossible that man is the boy's father. Henry Hewitt carries the mark of St. John!"

Henry looked back down at his toes. The mark of what?

"That can only mean," Sir Richard continued, pointing at Henry's father, "that you and your wife are the kidnappers, and judging from Snidefellow's hasty exit I should think he had something to do with it too."

Henry stared at his toes. What did Sir Richard mean, Bartholomew Hewitt was not his father?

Quite suddenly, Henry was swept into yards of silk. "Don't you see, Henry?" the duchess whispered in his ear. "Your six toes. That is the mark of a St. John. Not another family line in England carries it. Did you not know the truth when Sir Richard recovered the footprint?"

"N-no," Henry stuttered.

Sir Richard had come to stand next to the duchess. "I never showed it to him, Darla."

"Good grief," she said, "we might never have discovered it."

"Ah, I must argue that," Sir Richard said. "We might never have discovered it had Henry been less the boy than he is. He might have left me to my fate, you know. Instead, he sought to take my place on the scaffold. I imagine the duke would be proud."

Mr. Candlewick approached. "Well, well," he said, rubbing his hands together. "This is indeed an unexpected development. Fortunately, I know just what to do with it."

Mr. Candlewick addressed the magistrate in a loud voice. "Your Honor, the evidence will show the following: That the boy merely threw lime on the fly in a youthful attempt to help his benefactor. That the boy, unknown to anyone including himself, is the missing Lord William St. John. That the man posing as the boy's father is one of the kidnappers. The woman posing as his mother was also there on that horrific day and mistaken to be the shorter man. That Mr. Snidefellow is the third member of the conspiracy. And finally, that it would be most unfortunate if anyone else was suspected of being involved in the plot, due to their close relationship with the councilman."

The magistrate had a sickly look on his face. "I wasn't!" the magistrate cried. "I didn't know anything about it. I don't even like Snidefellow that much!"

"Very good," Mr. Candlewick said. "The best way for you to divorce yourself from this whole ugly business is to deliver a verdict. Quickly, man."

"Yes, quite right," the magistrate said. He jumped to his feet and banged his gavel. "This court finds that the boy is absolved from tampering with evidence, as it was only lime, and he is only a boy after all and . . . it turns out he is also the Duke of St. John. The defendant, Sir Richard Blackstone, is pronounced not guilty and further commended for returning the duchess's son." The magistrate pointed to the man and woman Henry had always known as his parents. "Lock those two up and go arrest Snidefellow while you're at it. This court is adjourned!"

The circuit prosecutor threw up his hands. "What just happened?"

Henry thought the same. What just happened?

It took Henry quite some time to fully comprehend what had occurred. Snidefellow had eluded the constable's pursuit and no one knew where he had gone. But the man and woman who had been the only parents Henry had ever known escaped the noose by making a full confession. Afterwards, they were put on a boat to Botany Bay. They would spend the rest of their lives as unpaid laborers in Australia.

The man who had posed as Henry's father was in truth named Bartholomew Hewitt and he was Snidefellow's brother-in-law. His wife, Druscilla Hewitt, was Snidefellow's sister. They all were very poor, but through some remote connection in the family, Snidefellow had been recommended for the councilman's position at Barton Commons. This gave all three of them high hopes of improving their lot in life. When Snidefellow arrived and saw that things were not to improve by much, he was furious. He had assumed he could make himself rich by issuing fines or demanding various kinds of payments. As it turned out, the villagers had little to give and it had been impossible to squeeze much out of them.

The three came up with the scheme to kidnap the duke's son and hold him for ransom. Once they had the silver, they would return the boy. Snidefellow would suddenly develop a health complaint and resign the position. They would take themselves abroad to Italy, buy a villa by the sea, and happily retire.

It had all gone wrong in the cave. Snidefellow hid in the shadows so he would not be recognized. But he had not hidden well enough. Once the duke spotted him, there was nothing left to do but kill him. Snidefellow struck the deadly blow.

After that, they changed their plan. They considered disposing of Henry, or even leaving him on a doorstep in Barton Commons, but in the end felt they'd better hold on

**184**

to him as a bargaining chip, should their plot ever be discovered. Snidefellow could not disappear without arousing suspicion, so they hid the silver and determined to bide their time until the kidnapping was long forgotten. But the duchess would not let it be forgotten. She kept an investigator on the case and there were times when Snidefellow felt the man got dangerously close to the truth.

Over the years, Snidefellow began to despair of ever being able to abscond with the silver. Until slowly he began to set his sights higher. Perhaps there was no need to run after all. He felt the duchess had become dependent on him as a counselor, and was that role so very far away from that of a husband? If they married, all of the duchess's wealth would be rightfully and legally his. The three had determined that there was no further value in holding on to Henry and had devised a plan to sell him off. It all could have gone off without a hitch had Sir Richard not hired him.

Snidefellow had always felt Sir Richard was dangerous; the duchess was too fond of him. But now, he'd brought the boy into their very neighborhood. Snidefellow saw an opportunity to rid himself of both of his problems after the strange events of the duchess's party. He would force Sir Richard and Henry to leave the county by accusing Sir Richard of witchcraft and painting Henry as an accomplice. After Sir Richard claimed to have seen a wolf, it was a simple matter to rile the villagers about a padfoot. But Sir Richard refused to leave. Instead, he proposed to the duchess and was accepted.

Snidefellow knew it was imperative that he get rid of Sir Richard before the marriage could take place. As he had already accused Sir Richard of witchcraft that seemed the simplest way to finally free himself of the knight. He had not thought he would actually have to conduct a trial—he had assumed throwing Sir Richard in jail and leaving the door unlocked would do the trick. Sir Richard would break out of prison and go abroad, taking Henry with him. But somehow, that blasted knight had never even bothered to try to open the latch.

When Snidefellow realized his strongbox full of letters had been stolen, he almost fled the county himself. He hid in the woods that first night, staring at his cottage and feeling sure someone would arrive to arrest him. When that didn't happen, he decided it had been taken by common thieves who had been disappointed that it only contained parchment and would not understand the cryptic communications between himself and Bartholomew Hewitt.

Neither the Crown nor the district council were aware that a trial was taking place because it was a staged fraud. Mr. Joswell, the supposed prosecutor, was a down-on-his-luck actor that Snidefellow had found in London. The man had been promised a share in the silver for his work. The trial was meant to force Sir Richard to flee when a guilty verdict was delivered and the knight truly believed he faced the gallows. Mr. Joswell had disappeared as quickly as he had arrived when he saw the plan had failed.

Snidefellow was dumbfounded over the sudden arrival

of a giant fly in the church. He told his brother-in-law that he was not the author of that trick, but thanks to the fly he felt assured that the guilty verdict would not arouse suspicion among the villagers. It was exactly the kind of proof they needed to see with their own eyes to believe Sir Richard guilty.

Snidefellow had determined that he would get rid of Henry one way or another, as nobody would miss a young urchin from London. If he could not sway the duchess to marry him, he would tell her he had to resign because of a broken heart. Either way, he would win. He would either marry the duchess and become a man with real power or he would at least be able to finally retrieve the silver. It seemed that nothing could go wrong until the fly suddenly shrank, and the boy decided to show everybody his toes.

Henry shivered when he considered all the years he had been their captive and not even known it. His instinct had been to run and so he had. He was lucky they had not managed to catch him.

The silver was finally recovered. It had been hidden in the valley that once housed Mary, Queen of Scots. Mr. Candlewick was paid handsomely and the rest was given to Fitzwilliam to finance another expedition to South America.

The tale of the recovered Duke of St. John spread throughout England. The queen herself requested to see Henry and spent nearly an hour questioning him about his experiences on the streets of London. At the end of it, she resolved to close the workhouses, demanded Parliament pass a law guarding the rights of children, and formed a council to develop more humane methods of helping her neediest citizens. She also conferred a knighthood on Mr. Clemens for the service he rendered to the Duke of St. John, by way of penny loaves.

Months later, the duchess, Sir Richard, and Henry sat in the duchess's drawing room after the wedding breakfast. They had decided to live in the duchess's manor, but would keep Blackstone Manor for Sir Richard's experiments. Much to Henry's surprise, his mother had not been against her husband continuing his attempts to invent something and she had even allowed Mary and Mr. Terrible to live in the house. She had put her foot down, though, about the piranhas. Sir Richard had built an aquarium, but it must remain in his old home.

They had decided weeks ago to give up the idea of calling Henry by his real name: William. Each time they had tried it, everybody kept forgetting, and the duchess was far too used to calling Billy Brash by William. He had been Henry all his life, and Henry he would stay.

Henry convinced his mother to promote Billy to be his companion. That meant Billy had a room next to Henry's and ate his meals with the family. He and Billy had the same taste in literature, so they stayed up late into the night, engrossed in stories of noble knights. Henry was teaching Billy to read so that he could begin taking a turn as the storyteller.

Henry stared down at his new boots. They had been specially made to accommodate his extra toes, just as the duke's had always been. Matilda and Harold rolled around the floor at his feet. Matilda had grown rapidly and Harold found that, these days, he could not win every contest.

"Now listen, you two," the duchess said to her new husband and her son, "we still haven't decided where we are going for our wedding trip. All we've managed to decide is that Bertram and Mrs. Splunket will care for Matilda and Harold while we are away."

"Bertram and Mrs. Splunket can be counted on to take good care of them while we're gone," Henry said. "I couldn't leave Matilda with anybody less reliable and still have a good time. I would be too worried and not even enjoy the scenery."

"Agreed," the duchess said, "but enjoy the scenery where?"

"There's always Italy," Sir Richard said.

"True," the duchess said. "So many people do go to Rome for a wedding trip."

"Rome would be a very appropriate place to go," Sir Richard said, nodding.

"Or," Henry said, hoping he could convince them of a rather brilliant idea that he and Billy had thought up, "it might be nice to go on a long cruise. I happen to know of a ship that is setting sail for South America in a week."

Sir Richard sat up. "Fitzwilliam's expedition! That's marvelous! I mean, no, for a wedding trip we probably should go to Rome."

"Rome is what most people do," the duchess said.

Henry had gotten to know his mother better over the months. He did not believe she wanted to go to Italy and sit around in the sunshine or tour cathedrals or wander around museums. He said, "South America would be full of adventure. We might find ourselves lost in the jungle, or fighting off a jaguar, or even wrestling a crocodile."

"Wrestling a crocodile," the duchess murmured. "We could not do *that* in Rome."

"And," Henry continued, this time directing his appeal to Sir Richard, "who knows what kind of creatures and plants we could bring back. Your dream of a hybrid rose fly eliminator might not be dead after all. We really can't know until we get there."

"The Blackstone Fly Eliminator," Sir Richard murmured.

The duchess leapt to her feet and said, "South America it is. But we go only under one condition. We do not bring home any spiders."

Henry smiled. He was about to be anchorless again. But this time, he wouldn't mind floating around.

# ACKNOWLEDGMENTS

As with most books, this one would never have lived any-where but inside my own computer without aid arriving from every direction. From my editor, Adrienne Szpyrka, seeing what the book could be before it was quite there, to Brigadoon (otherwise known as Vermont College of Fine Arts), to the Dedications (my partners in crime and go-to people for all things literature), thanks to the many hands that helped.

# ABOUT THE AUTHOR

Lisa Doan has an MFA in Writing for Children and Young Adults from Vermont College of Fine Arts, sits on the board of the Brandywine Valley Writer's Group, and is the author of the award-winning middle grade series *The Berenson Schemes*.

She is a dual citizen of the United States and Ireland and has traveled and lived in Africa, Asia, and Central America. Operating under the idea that life is short, her occupations have included: master SCUBA diving instructor, New York City headhunter, owner-chef of a restaurant in the Caribbean, television show set medic, and Deputy Prothonotary of a county court. She currently lives in West Chester, Pennsylvania, and works in social services.

Connect with Lisa at lisadoan.org, facebook.com/lisadoanauthor and twitter.com/LisaADoan.